Wolf! Wolf!

"My dear Phyllis," it began, "you will be glad to hear that the operation on my varicose veins has gone off successfully. Now I have to get up and walk the length of the corridor outside my ward every few hours and not stand still at all, but if I stop, mark time while I talk to anyone. . . .

"Imagine my surprise, shock really and horror, too, when this afternoon on my last trudge up the corridor, with my legs—all covered with little wounds, you know—smarting like nobody's business, I saw two men standing outside the glass door and just beside the lift, where the notice says 'Please Walk Down.' They had on dark suits and each of them had a case of some sort. Then one of them turned and it was THE BLACK CAT!"

Tom looked up again.

"Black Cat?" he asked, with a puzzled frown. "Should I know? Television character?"

"Forgotten already? Our very well-known local murderer, went about killing old ladies in the late fifties. Picked up near here in the end and put away for life."

"Then how—?"

"Let out two years ago."

Other titles in the Walker British Mystery Series

Peter Alding • MURDER IS SUSPECTED
Peter Alding • RANSOM TOWN
Jeffrey Ashford • SLOW DOWN THE WORLD
Jeffrey Ashford • THREE LAYERS OF GUILT
Pierre Audemars • NOW DEAD IS ANY MAN
Marion Babson • DANGEROUS TO KNOW
Marion Babson • THE LORD MAYOR OF DEATH
Brian Ball • MONTENEGRIN GOLD
Josephine Bell • A QUESTION OF INHERITANCE
Josephine Bell • TREACHERY IN TYPE
Josephine Bell • VICTIM
W. J. Burley • DEATH IN WILLOW PATTERN
W. J. Burley • TO KILL A CAT
Desmond Cory • THE NIGHT HAWK
Desmond Cory • UNDERTOW
John Creasey • THE BARON AND THE UNFINISHED PORTRAIT
John Creasey • HELP FROM THE BARON
John Creasey • THE TOFF AND THE FALLEN ANGELS
John Creasey • TRAP THE BARON
June Drummond • FUNERAL URN
June Drummond • SLOWLY THE POISON
William Haggard • THE NOTCH ON THE KNIFE
William Haggard • THE POISON PEOPLE
William Haggard • TOO MANY ENEMIES
William Haggard • VISA TO LIMBO
William Haggard • YESTERDAY'S ENEMY
Simon Harvester • MOSCOW ROAD
Simon Harvester • ZION ROAD
J. G. Jeffreys • SUICIDE MOST FOUL
J. G. Jeffreys • A WICKED WAY TO DIE
J. G. Jeffreys • THE WILFUL LADY
Elizabeth Lemarchand • CHANGE FOR THE WORSE
Elizabeth Lemarchand • STEP IN THE DARK
Elizabeth Lemarchand • SUDDENLY WHILE GARDENING
Elizabeth Lemarchand • UNHAPPY RETURNS
Laurie Mantell • A MURDER OR THREE
John Sladek • BLACK AURA
John Sladek • INVISIBLE GREEN

JOSEPHINE BELL
Wolf! Wolf!

WALKER AND COMPANY · NEW YORK

Copyright © 1979 by D. B. Ball

All rights reserved. No part of this book may be reproduced or transmitted in any form or by any means, electric or mechanical, including photocopying, recording, or by any information storage and retrieval system, without permission in writing from the Publisher.

All the characters and events portrayed in this story are fictitious.

First published in the United States of America in 1980 by the Walker Publishing Company, Inc.

This paperback edition first published in 1984.

ISBN: 0-8027-3077-9

Library of Congress Catalog Card Number: 80-51993

Printed in the United States of America

10 9 8 7 6 5 4 3 2 1

1

The two men met on the landing beside the head of the stairs and the doors of the lifts. The younger of the two, upstanding, well built, active, had mounted the two flights briskly. The older, broadened into middle age, permanently red-faced, had chosen the lift, self-operated.

They exchanged a rapid glance of recognition, but their attention was given more precisely to the two corridors that led away behind glass doors on each side of the landing. Hospital corridors, made evident by an occasional trolley, empty of content, and a wheel-chair standing askew under one of the row of windows that gave light from the wall opposite the stairs and lifts.

The place was part of the Isobel Saunders Hospital, subscribed for and erected in memory of a local benefactor when the area was still sufficiently separated from the nearby city to be named and ruled a town rather than a suburb. It was built in late Victorian brick as a cottage hospital, enlarged to two storeys under Edward VII as part beneficiary of the fund raised in his name, and in 1948 taken over in its now crowded surroundings as part of the National Health Service.

Development had not stopped there. The area was

conveniently close to the main ring-road extension that disposed of through traffic at great speed, but with a corresponding increase in the number of accidents. A new casualty admission ward was needed with more wards above for the very seriously injured. This extension was built rather slowly and at greatly increasing cost during the next ten years, but by the early seventies lack of funds, shortage of nurses and of those consultants highly qualified enough to deal with modern injuries, had caused a good deal of change in the new department. On the whole there were fewer fractures; head injuries, spinal injuries, severe burns, needed intensive care for which the Isobel Saunders was not equipped. Otherwise glass cuts, bruises, together with emotional shock might be dealt with in casualty or as part of general surgery, now in its more chronic or less urgent form filling the waiting lists.

This decline was very marked at the Isobel Saunders Hospital. Those empty corridors on either side of the landing on the second floor were typical and known to be so. Therefore the two men, meeting with the briefest recognition, moved quickly to a door opposite the lift, gave a rapid look to right and left, unlocked it with a key held by the older man and passed inside.

This older man was carrying a brief case, the younger a more substantial carrier that held normally some of the aids to his profession, that of architect. The former looked about him, for the place was quite empty except for one old, small table against a wall, under the only natural source of light, a small window. There were cupboards up to the ceiling on one side of the room, another door at the other. There were two small upright chairs.

"Doesn't look like anything much happens in here," he said, growling his criticism.

"Nor it does," said the younger one. "That's why I suggested—"

"Quite. Quite."

The red-faced man had unfastened his brief case and was taking out a number of large envelopes. The other, his eyes fixed upon them, his face grim but expectant, drew nearer.

"Six," said the older man, holding out the envelopes.

"Can I count—?"

"Be your age! Securities. You'd need a trunk for notes. Haven't you made arrangements?"

The younger man flushed. His attempt at ignorance had failed. He realised he was not, as he had thought, dealing with local talent, but someone experienced, possibly dangerous. Too late now to draw back: besides the deed was done: this was the reward.

Too late indeed. The envelopes were held out to him, his hand was already grasping them, when a small high unfamiliar voice met them like the lash of a thin whip.

"For me, too, please."

They swung round, each dropping his hand so that the envelopes fell to the floor between them. The closed door on the other side of the room was open and in the frame of it, standing against the blackness beyond was a small figure in a nurse's uniform, white apron over soothing green, white cap on blue-black hair, small tanned hand stretched out.

She moved forward a little. Her smooth cream-yellow face held no fear, no expression whatever. But her small black eyes had a greedy gleam in them.

"For me, too, please," she repeated.

Neither man moved, but their eyes met. Then the older man smiled.

"Where did you spring from?" he asked, genially.

She did not answer, but continued, with hand outstretched, to repeat her request.

The younger man said, "It's a big cupboard. Been empty since the last re-organisation of these wards. Used to store trolleys and wheel-chairs in the old days."

"Didn't you look?" asked the other, still holding the little nurse's attention with his red-faced smile.

"Money for me, please," she said, in the same high mechanical voice.

"Backsheesh, eh?"

"I no understand."

"Not your lingo? But they know what it is in Hong Kong, don't they?"

Her face twisted suddenly. She spat sideways. The men laughed.

"So much for the Chinks, eh?"

Keeping his eyes on the girl he said, without altering the tone of his voice, "Better see if there's any more of this lot in that cupboard you said was empty."

"It was empty," the younger man insisted. "I checked yesterday. Couldn't very well dodge about in here today as well, could I?"

But he moved away and searched the dark cupboard, switching on the light, which worked, he noticed, a thing he had not observed the day before. It worked now and it showed the bare space he had noted the day before, but at the end of it a pile of rugs and cushions, the significance of which together with the presence of the girl, was quite sufficiently obvious.

When he came out he switched off the light and shut the door. He was now behind the girl, who was still facing the older man. He saw the envelopes lying on the floor beyond her. A sudden fury swept over him. They are mine, he swore to himself. After all I've done, the risks, the troubles—

His eyes met those of his paymaster. There was no need of words between them.

2

"Oh, no!"

Phyllis Hunt thrust a letter at her husband, who put out a hand for it without taking his eyes from the newspaper propped up before him.

"No, what?" Tom Hunt's interest was minimal.

"Read it. Aunt Amy off again!"

"But she's in hospital, isn't she?"

"As if that would stop her! Or even slow her down. Read it!"

Having wrenched his attention from the world news to attach it to Aunt Amy, Phyllis re-filled both their coffee cups and sat back to observe Tom's reaction. It was curt, but spoken mildly.

"The woman's mad, of course."

"We've known that for years. It doesn't help to repeat it every time. What do we do?"

"You mean what do *you* do? She's *your* aunt, not mine, thank God."

"Coward! Honestly, Tom, it could be more than a nuisance, with her in the Isobel Saunders. She's actually proposing to go to the police with this discovery, as she calls it."

Tom had folded up the letter to hand it back to his

wife, but now he unfolded it again and read it more carefully.

'My dear Phyllis,' it began, 'you will be glad to hear that the operation on my varicose veins has gone off successfully, or so they tell me, in spite of the fact that it was hellishly painful as soon as I came out of the anaesthetic, so they put me under again at once and it wasn't too bad when they let me come round the second time. Now I have to get up and walk the length of the corridor outside my ward every few hours and not stand still at all, but if I stop, mark time while I talk to anyone.'

"She does go on about the op., doesn't she?" Tom grumbled. "I nearly gave up when I reached the end of all that, but there's screeds more."

"Persevere," Phyl encouraged him. "You are getting now to what they call the nub."

Tom grunted but returned to the letter.

'Imagine my surprise, shock really and horror, too, when this afternoon on my last trudge up the corridor, with my legs – all covered with little wounds, you know – smarting like nobody's business, I saw two men standing outside the glass door and just beside the lift, where the notice says Please Walk Down. They had on dark suits and each of them had a case of some sort. Then one of them turned and it was THE BLACK CAT!'

Tom looked up again.

"Black Cat?" he asked, with a puzzled frown. "Should I know? Television character?"

"Forgotten already? Our very well-known local murderer, went about killing old ladies in the late fifties. Picked up near here in the end and put away for life."

"Then how—?"

"Let out two years ago."

"You're very up to date with the villain's biography."

"Aunt Amy is, you mean. Read on."

'I was flabbergasted. I stood, frozen with horror until I remembered my treatment and started to mark time furiously to make up for standing still. He rushed away down the stairs.'

Tom exploded into wild laughter.

"Aunt Amy with her prominent eyes and a white face, doing knees up on the other side of a glass door. The poor chap must have thought he'd hit the loony bin."

"Your coffee's getting cold," Phyl said icily.

Tom drank, nodded and finished reading the letter.

'Nobody seems to know who these two men were or what they were doing on the second floor of the Isobel Saunders. General surgery I understand, mostly of a chronic, repair or remedial nature. Like my veins. But I'm quite sure I was not mistaken. I cut out and kept all the photographs in the newspapers. I suppose I ought to report it to the police. What do you think?'

Tom handed the letter back.

"Bonkers, as I said before. The cat murderer, can't remember his real name, was in his late thirties when he was put away, so he would be nearly sixty. I don't believe he could possibly look the same now as he did then. But you'll have to stop her going to the Law, won't you?"

"I'll try. I was going to see her today, anyhow. They'll let her out soon, I suppose. Would it be a good thing as well as kind, to ask her here for a few days?"

Tom groaned but he saw the point.

"Keep her under control, you mean? O.K. if we must. Your best deeds always work well in both directions, don't they, darling?"

"Beast," Phyl said, getting up to kiss him fondly.

The Hunts lived in a village in the country, now almost a suburb of the small town of Newchester, where Tom worked as junior partner in a firm of chartered accountants. It was about ten miles from the Isobel Saunders Hospital and as that establishment had been already swallowed up by urban sprawl, so Newchester, their town, threatened the village, Newchest Polegate, with a council estate and an even more unwelcome string of separate eccentrically designed larger dwellings, whose infant gardens could not yet hide their unrural shapes. However, as Tom said to himself each time he passed them on his way to his office, 'new customers for us with any luck.'

He said it now, driving past one of the less offensive buildings. He remembered that it did indeed house a client of the firm, one with interesting, if not distressing, accountancy problems, a consultant surgeon, already a pleasant acquaintance, a potential friend.

Stimulated perhaps by the breakfast conversation with Phyl about her Aunt Amy's present experiences in hospital, Tom looked up the Beddoes' file later that day. He was curious to discover where Michael actually worked, presumably within a fairly short distance of their village. Newchester has a general hospital that still stood where the Victorians had built it, in the centre of the former working class area, still a welter of decaying factories, with long terraces of slums, partly demolished, partly over-crowded by a mixed population. But not very readily accessible from his own and the surgeon's side.

Tom was not surprised then to find that in addition to his post at the Newchester General, a fully part-time appointment, which meant a mixture of N.H.S. sessions and private practice, Michael Beddoes also served the Isobel Saunders, which still stoutly upheld its right to have fee-paying beds as laid down in its founding charter in terms the bureaucrats had not yet been able to get round.

So Beddoes might be a useful source of internal information on the Isobel Saunders if that should be called for by any future trouble over Aunt Amy, whose name, Tom had long ago decided, was bother, nuisance, exasperation, farce, if not real trouble itself.

Phyl, that same morning, disposed of the routine housework, checked the fridge and the deep freeze for any necessary additions she ought to get in Newchester and started off in her own small Mini van. Aunt Amy was a bore, but she had been Phyl's mother's favourite sister, unwisely encouraged to follow a training in dramatic art with no real talent but an overpowering energy and enthusiasm. After years of struggle with inevitable disappointment she had given up the stage for the lecture theatre platform. Here her very lively delivery and unusual point of view on most of the classics made her quite popular with the Women's Institute and kindred bodies. Also with the Drama Clubs of the smaller village variety. She earned very little money, spent freely when she did have any and relied, with real but astonishing innocence upon her family to continue to support her. As they unfailingly did until the last of them, Phyl's mother, knew she was dying.

"Amy won't have anyone now," Phyl's mother told her. "I can't expect you to take my place, you have your own family. You don't, you can't possibly, feel as I do about Amy. But it isn't all nonsense, you know, this longing for drama, this thirst for excitement. She does have intuitions or whatever they are. It might get her into trouble. I mean real trouble; danger even. These days that doesn't sound like the nonsense it would have been when I was young. Life *is* more dangerous."

"I'll keep an eye on her," Phyllis promised. And she had kept her word, often reluctantly, with an exasperated sense of duty. Sometimes, as this morning, with a sense of the ridiculous. Aunt Amy, marking time on behalf of her veins as she thought she recognised, through a hospital ward's glass door, the face of a notorious murderer.

The Isobel Saunders Hospital, formerly a cherished semi-charitable institution had earlier in the century been treated as something special, part private nursing home, part geriatric retreat, at fees the impoverished retired professional and upper middle class could afford. Well-bred and knowledgeable trained women had supplied Sisters for the wards, headed by a Matron, often with aristocratic connections, one of that plethora of women the First World War had deprived of their future husbands, before conscription had done the same thing for the population in general.

But now, struggling under the weight of at least one tier too many of ignorant civil servants, added to public employees intent only on promoting their own positions and salaries, the atmosphere had changed, sadly, disastrously, changed. No longer Matron, but Nursing Officer No. 7, ruled the former body of caring, skilled women, carrying out treatment ordered by their superiors in medical knowledge and skill, the consultants. Formerly authority had been accepted because it was understood as natural coming from a higher source. Not regarded, as now, a tyranny to be resented and resisted at all cost.

Phyl, passing an individual in the entrance hall, dressed in a tweed suit with collar and tie, whom she took to be the door porter, said, "I have come to see my aunt, Miss Amy Tupper. Can you tell me where to find her, please? It's a private room, I think."

"Second floor," the man said, waving an arm towards the stairs before immediately resuming his conversation with a man in a rather grubby long white coat.

Phyllis mounted. Probably she would have taken the lift, but she had not wanted to ask that very uninterested person in the tweed suit just where the lift doors were and whether the lift was self-operated or not.

There was no one to be seen on the landing of the first floor. Hoping her brief direction was correct she moved past the central lift doors and mounted again. At the second floor landing another empty silent space lay before her. While she looked about a short plump girl in uniform came through the glass door on her left.

"I am looking for Miss Tupper, nurse," she said, panting a little, for it had been quite a steep climb. "Can you tell me—?"

But the girl, her small face expressionless, had moved to the opposite door and passed through it.

Angry now, Phyl pushed through the left hand glass door and marched along the corridor, determined to find her aunt however unwilling the so-called 'service' was to help her.

In the end she did so. An older woman, whom she

took to be the Sister of the ward got up from the table in her small cubby-hole of an office, open to the corridor, and came to the door.

"Miss Tupper? Varicose veins operation. Yes. On the right, third door from the end. Due to leave us tomorrow. – Oh, very satisfactory. You are her niece?"

"Yes, I am. Sorry to bother you," Phyl said, looking past the woman at the pile of paper on her small desk. "I tried to ask a nurse who was crossing the landing but she didn't seem to hear or even see me."

A faint shade crossed Sister's face, but she smiled.

"Their English isn't very good," she said. "Some of them I mean. You'll find Miss Tupper—"

"Yes. Thank you."

Phyl hurried away up the corridor. Poor Sister. Stuck with all those forms and reports. Obviously no time for her nurses or no wish to tangle with them. What a change from the old days.

Not so old, either. She remembered the devoted care at the great teaching hospital where her mother had suffered her last operation and had not been able to recover from it. The care, the kindness, the sympathy, the understanding, from the whole well-knit staff, from the liftman to the ward cleaner, the telephone operator, the operating theatre porter, all these working in the same spirit as the purely medical side—

She reached the end of the ward without seeing Aunt Amy's name on any door, then moved back slowly. Third from the end, that harrassed Sister had told her. She knocked and entered boldly.

Aunt Amy was sitting up in bed, half-dressed, with her bandaged legs straight out before her on top of the bed-clothes.

"Welcome, welcome, my dear child! When did you get my letter?"

"Only this morning. How are you?"

"Two days, in spite of the ninepenny stamp! Me? Perfectly all right, of course. They want to throw me out tomorrow, but I'm not going till I've decided how to deal with my outstanding discovery. Don't you find it astounding?"

"I'm interested in your legs, Aunt Amy. Much more important than noticing a supposed likeness—"

"*Supposed!* I'm *sure*. It can't have been anyone else!"

"But Tom says—"

"Tom always shoots me down, bless his legal heart."

"Not legal. Mathematical, if you like."

"Much the same. Accountants have to know a lot of law, anyhow, to be able to fiddle their clients' tax dues."

It was yet another repetition of an old old argument. Phyl looked round for a chair and sat down. She remembered at last the grapes she had been carrying all this time and got up again to present them.

"I didn't expect them to let you out under a fortnight," she said. "But when they do won't you come to us for a bit of convalescence? Tom said to insist on that unless you had more attractive plans."

Aunt Amy laughed.

"Good for Tom. I bet he can think of many more attractive plans than having his scatty old aunt by marriage rushing off on another red herring trail. He'd be wrong, though. I told you and I mean to follow it up. That dreadful murderer was let out two years ago and when he saw I recognised him he dashed away, so he may have been at his appalling work again."

"But how? Where? In this hospital? The day before yesterday."

"Why not? It was old ladies before. The other ward on this floor is geriatric, mixed male and female, separate rooms, like this. Mostly N.H.S., a few private patients, but most of the fee-paying beds have been done away with."

"All right, but two days ago, when you wrote to me. And there has been no dreadful news of a death at the Isobel Saunders, has there? Surely it would be discovered and the alarm raised before the man even left the hospital? On your own floor, too. What time did you see him?"

"Afternoon. In visiting hours. About now, it could be. Tea time, in fact."

As if to confirm her words the door opened and a stout elderly woman in a long white overall carried in a tray with a cup of tea, poured out, strong, with two lumps of sugar in the saucer, together with a small plate bearing a thinly buttered half scone and a sweet biscuit.

"Ready for your tea, love?" inquired the stout woman cheerfully.

"What about another cup for my niece?" asked Aunt Amy.

Before the elderly attendant could answer Phyl got up briskly. "Thank you, no," she said, to the woman's evident relief. "No, I must be off. I have the car in the official park and my time must be running out. Ten pence an hour here. And a keen looking warden on the approach road as I drove in."

She bent to kiss her aunt.

"Do come to us when they let you out," she said. "Truly we'd love to have you. Lots of nice country walks for those miles they make you do and a long chair in the garden to put the legs up on, if it's warm enough. Promise."

"I'll think about it," Aunt Amy agreed. "I'd certainly like to be somewhere not too far away. In case. You know what I mean."

"Yes, of course," Phyl told her.

Tom got home earlier than usual that evening, but instead of the cheerful shout which usually announced such an exceptional release from toil he came in so quickly and silently that Phyl shot into the hall from the kitchen, half afraid it was a stranger she had heard arrive.

His face was enough. She only had time to say quickly "What's happened?" before she saw he was holding out a newspaper.

"Did you listen to the news at five o'clock?"

"No. I never do."

"Read that!"

She did not have to read. The words sprang at her from the front page of an evening paper, huge black words.

BODY OF STRANGLED NURSE FOUND IN HOSPITAL STORE.

At the Isobel Saunders Hospital this afternoon—

Phyl dropped the paper.

"But I was *there* this afternoon. To see Aunt Amy. It's not *possible!* When—?"

"My girl at the office had been given the paper by the messenger boy. I was nearly through for the day. I wondered why you hadn't phoned, or if you were held up there with Aunt Amy."

"But nothing was going on there, no emergency, I mean, no commotion. All peaceful and pretty depressing, I may say. Aunt Amy's fine, walking around and talking – But my God, *was she right this time!*"

Tom drew a deep breath.

"She'll know what's happened by now and she'll be damned sure she's right."

"It's incredible! She said she would wait a few days to tell the police she'd seen that man."

"She won't have had to wait. They'll be taking statements from every soul in the place."

"She said she'd like to come here tomorrow when they proposed to let her out. She wanted to be near the hospital, but not in it when she spoke to the police."

They heard a car come into their drive and draw up outside.

"That's a taxi," Tom said, turning to face the door.

They heard voices; a woman's and an answering man.

"It's Aunt Amy," Phyl said.

It was.

3

Aunt Amy marched up to the front door of her niece's house and stood there, having pressed the bell push, marking time. The taxi driver, who had followed with her bag, stood waiting for his fare, which she assembled from her handbag, still marking time with her feet. When Phyllis opened the door she stepped forward, while the taxi driver, who had expected a larger tip and now regretted leaving his cab to help the old bag, muttered a rude complaint and turned away.

"Sorry to plant myself on you without notice," Aunt Amy said cheerfully. "Wanted to get away before the police started work. You've heard what happened there today, haven't you?"

"Phyl hadn't," Tom said, meeting Aunt Amy at the door of the sitting room. "My office had the first radio account and then the evening papers, of course. But do come in."

"You ought to put the legs up, oughtn't you?" Phyl urged. "Try the sofa, or would you rather have two chairs?"

Aunt Amy tossed the sofa cushions together in a heap at one end of it and sank down with a grateful sigh.

"Wonderful," she said. "No lumps, like that hospital bed."

She beamed at the two puzzled faces.

"You're wondering why they let me out, with the truly startling news I've got for them. Well—"

"You don't mean to say you haven't *seen* the police yet?"

"Seen, but not spoken to. Now just listen and I'll explain."

It was going to take time, Tom decided, so he found a chair for himself. Phyl, after a rapid mental review of her cooking arrangements for the dinner that evening, decided there would be enough for her aunt without making drastic changes and sat down herself.

"It was on my walk up the corridor about five o'clock," Aunt Amy began. "I'd had my tea, as you know, Phyllis, and Mrs. Walls had taken away the tray. Just as I got to the glass door at the end of the ward I heard a loud confused squeaking of high voices and I saw three little nurses burst out of the double door opposite the lift. It's a big store room. I had looked into it when the door had been left open by those two men. It was usually locked, but I think there are keys available for the nursing staff and for the porters, I suppose. It was nearly empty. There were cupboards on the walls but I didn't try to look into them. There was an inner door, a big cupboard or small room, it could be, but this was locked."

Aunt Amy paused, looking thoughtful.

"That was on the day of my first day of walking, the same day that I saw the murderer; in the afternoon I went into the store room when I found the door unlocked."

"What happened today was in the late afternoon

though, wasn't it?" Tom said, to recall his wife's aunt to the present excitement.

"I don't know *when* the wretched girl was killed," Aunt Amy protested. "I'm only telling you about the place where she was found by those three little nurses."

"Sorry. Go on."

"They always talk to each other in their own lingo," Aunt Amy explained. "It's not Chinese, they always say they don't like the Chinese, but I expect it's something like it. Far Eastern, anyhow. They'll have had their nursing training, such as it is, here, so they all manage English for the patients. They're pleasant enough to look at, very clean, very neat and tidy, well combed hair, but rather heartless, I find. But then the whole Health Service has stopped being geared to patients' needs, except by the senior medical staff and—"

"What were the Far Eastern nurses squeaking about?" Tom asked.

Phyl had already slipped away to the kitchen.

"Their murdered colleague, of course," said Aunt Amy.

"Discovered in that store room?"

"In the inner cupboard or room. It used to hold wheel-chairs, theatre trolleys and stretchers, I believe. But the orthopaedic and casualty theatres are on the first floor now, in a new extension. Very up to date, but often out of use when the porters are on strike or there isn't an anaesthetist available for the surgeon."

"So the girls ran out screeching. What then?"

"They burst into my corridor and ran past me to find Sister, I suppose. We do have a young woman I call Sister, Irish, very competent, in her thirties, I imagine. She never complains about the foreign staff, but you can tell sometimes by the way she looks at them. She scares them, but not too much. They don't make mistakes over doses in her wards. She has both wards on the second floor."

"What did you do when the nurses ran past you?"

"Turned and walked after them. They did find Sister and she came out of her office and they all passed me as I walked back to my room. They were trying to explain something to her in English slowly and very carefully. They were repeating a name, over and over. Tan Sunee."

"The name of the nurse found strangled?" said Tom.

"Yes."

Aunt Amy went on with her story. It took a long time. Phyl was able to make up a bed in the spare room for her aunt, in the intervals of cooking the dinner, while Tom continued to listen, fascinated by the persistence and inspired timing that had enabled Aunt Amy to arrive on her scheduled walk at the lift landing and ward door exactly at the moment when a stretcher with its burden covered by a sheet was wheeled out to the lift, pushed by a hospital porter and flanked by two uniformed policemen.

Upon seeing the lift door open to receive them all she had gone back to her room, dressed quickly, and without saying goodbye to anyone, picked up her hastily filled soft bag and made her way to the door of the hospital.

"I had my discharge in my handbag," she explained to Tom, "I would have rung you in the evening, as it might be now, to ask if I might come. But I didn't produce my surgeon's paper. There were police in the hall. They stopped me, so I just said, 'Canteen.

Voluntary.' and they let me go. I walked to the end of the street, only a few yards, turned the corner out of sight and picked up a taxi in a very few minutes. And here I am."

"Here you are," said Tom, admiringly. "But you'll have to explain to the police. Going off like that, on a pretty blatant lie, won't have done you any good with them. Why did you?"

"Why did I do what?"

"Tell a lie to get away from the hospital?"

"Because that murderer – Tilsett, he was called, wasn't he? – because, as I explained to you, he'd seen that I recognised him. I told you."

Phyllis, who had re-entered the room in time to hear this speech said, "Tom is sure you must have been mistaken. He thinks Tilsett, only out of the nick two years ago after years and years inside, couldn't possibly still look like the Black Cat of those old newspaper photographs."

"He looked at me," Aunt Amy said obstinately. "He saw that I recognised him, he stared at me and turned and ran down the stairs."

"You'll have to tell the police," said Tom. "As soon as possible, too."

"I'm quite aware of that. I want to meet them. I did *not* want to risk anyone getting at me in the Isobel Saunders. The hospital hasn't got this address, only my own home one."

"Then let Phyl take you up to your room while I try to arrange for the Law to come here to see you."

Detective Superintendent Robertson was surprisingly grateful for Tom's call. The latter had been persuaded to delay it until after the three of them had eaten the excellent dinner Phyl had provided with such speed and ingenuity. He came to their house less than an hour after getting the call, accompanied by Detective Sergeant Craig. He did not at once explain the reason for his gratitude. On the contrary he listened to Aunt Amy's story with a frowning concentration that might have put off a less ebullient spirit.

She repeated her tale, Tom noted, in very nearly the same words she had used to himself earlier. This seemed to make it more believable, though he still could not but doubt the identity of the man she believed she recognised.

"You saw two men on the landing?" the Superintendent asked. "You did not see them come out of the store room?"

"Not actually leave the room. But I knew they had been into it."

"How did you know that?"

"Because they had not really shut the door. Those men, I mean. It was only closed. It was nearly always kept locked."

"So you don't really *know* if they had been *in* the store room?"

"I am sure they had been from the way they were standing. They must have been."

"Why must they?"

Aunt Amy's face grew pink, her lips trembled.

"Because they weren't in my corridor as I walked towards the landing and they weren't in the other corridor, which you can see dimly across the landing. All plain glass. Cheaper, I suppose."

"The men," said the Superintendent, recalling her fron the threatened digression. "If they were nowhere to be seen as you approached, but were there, near the lift when you arrived, how is it you didn't see them leave the store room, only a couple of yards away?"

Aunt Amy considered.

"I don't really know," she said frankly at last. "I concluded they had been in the store room when I suddenly saw them."

"Both of them? You suddenly saw both?"

"Yes. Definitely, both."

"You are implying, with your stated recognition of a known criminal, that he may have been responsible for this killing? Are you implying that both men were responsible? Or that one merely watched the other and took no action to prevent it or report it afterwards?"

Aunt Amy faltered. She was quite aware of the flimsy nature of her evidence, its obvious imperfections, but she was unwilling to acknowledge this. Her face took on a closed look, familiar to the detective.

"About the unshut door," he began.

"Not unshut. Unlocked." Aunt Amy took pleasure in correcting him.

"You tried it then?"

"Of course. The Black Cat had run off down the stairs, the other man walked away into the ward, so when they had both gone I went out on the landing, tried the store room door, found it was unlocked and looked in. But I didn't *go* in, of course. Or rather, only just inside. It was quite empty. The inner door, which I took to be a cupboard, was shut."

"You are sure you didn't go right inside the store room?"

"Quite sure."

"Nevertheless, Miss Tupper, I must ask you to give me your fingerprints. Sergeant!"

"Yes, sir."

Thoroughly pleased with the developing drama, Aunt Amy submitted to the routine finger-printing. She went on with her story while Detective Sergeant Craig performed.

"I told Sister about the door being unlocked," she explained. "I think she went along to see to it, but the paper says it was some nurses, friends of the dead girl, who found her body today. Not Sister, two days ago. Could she?"

"We do not yet know when this girl died," Robertson said coldly. "The postmortem report is not in yet."

"You mean?" Aunt Amy was quite taken aback. "But that makes my evidence a nonsense?"

"You have given no evidence, only a very far-fetched theory," Robertson told her. He was getting rather tired of Aunt Amy. "Our enquiries at the hospital have only just begun. We are interviewing all who knew the girl, foreign workers and British alike, fellow workers of all kinds, as well as outside friends and relations."

Detective Sergeant Craig had finished his work and packed up the results with his apparatus. Both men got to their feet.

"I'm sorry you saw fit to jump the gun in taking your discharge from the hospital, Miss Tupper," Robertson said. "But I understand the shock of the event and your identification of a known criminal you allege was present in the building two days ago may have upset your judgment—"

"My judgment operated quite normally and I was not in a state of shock. I acted in reasonable self-protection."

The Detective Superintendent did not argue the

point. Besides, this interview had been unexpectedly productive. He wanted to pursue one or two new ideas at the Isobel Saunders. They could wait until the next day when he would have the results of the postmortem. Apart from Miss Tupper's crazy idea about Tilsett, the over-dramatised, so-called Black Cat, it was obvious that the old lady could have taken no part in the murder. True, she had looked into the main part of the store room, but she had not, or said she had not, looked into the little inner store where the body had been found. So she was no help in discovering whether by that time the victim had been strangled or not. At least the outer door had been open and Miss Tupper said she had reported the fact to Sister Byrnes, who was in charge of both parts of the second floor ward.

But Sister Byrnes had not passed on that fact to him. Not important enough? Or too important from her personal point of view? He would have to talk to Sister again; clear up the present confusion over access to that store room. How many keys to it were available? Who had them? Was it supposed to be always kept locked? If so, why, when nothing of any importance to the hospital was any longer kept there?

He would learn the answers to these questions in the morning. More important now was the problem of the dead girl's boy-friend, named by her fellow nurses, absent from the hospital on sick leave for the last two days, but working at his usual job of assistant pharmacist in the hospital dispensary before that.

He had been missing from his bed at his lodgings that evening, following the discovery of the murder. A search had been set up immediately in the neighbourhood, not easy in the crowded, immigrant community to which he belonged and who wished to have nothing whatever to do with the Law. The boy-friend was naturally the routine first suspect; his behaviour so far had been a routine disappearance.

On their way back to Newchester Police Station the two detectives had news of the young man. It came over their car radio.

Ali Ahmed had been picked up at an eating house where he usually took any meals he did not get at the hospital canteen. He had submitted to the police invitation to make a statement of his doings for the last week. He was waiting for Detective Superintendent Robertson's return. He looked ill, the Station Officer said, but resigned.

"Bloody obstinate, I don't mind betting," Robertson grumbled and gave an order to treat the bugger very carefully. "Most likely an open and shut case," he added to Craig, who was driving. "Pharmacist, is he? Must know enough English to do without an interpreter. Surely those chaps who call themselves 'authorities' wouldn't be damned stupid enough to engage a dope pusher or addict or one who might actually *poison* a patient?"

"It happens all the same," said the Detective Sergeant. "It was on the box—"

"Forget it," said Robertson.

They drove on in silence.

4

To Robertson's relief Ali Ahmed spoke English fluently, with a characteristic accent. He gave his country of origin as Pakistan and agreed that his work permit for five years had been granted after his permit to study Pharmacology had been successful in gaining him the necessary qualification to practise the dispensing of drugs. He had been appointed assistant pharmacist at the Isobel Saunders a year ago. He had found the post interesting and satisfying. He had not yet made up his mind whether or not he wanted to stay in England or return to his own country.

"You have friends here among your own people?" the detective asked him.

"Yes. Naturally."

"Your doctor seems to be a countryman."

Robertson turned over the certificate of illness Ahmed had produced from his pocket when he was picked up.

"Naturally," the pharmacist repeated, adding, "It was not severe. A liver chill."

"As well as those friends of your own race you no doubt have made friends with fellow workers at the hospital?"

"Naturally."

This parrot cry, as Robertson regarded it, annoyed him unreasonably. He decided to pass on, even at risk of appearing to bully the little chap. For Ali Ahmed was not a robust specimen: he was small-boned, narrow-faced, about as dark, but no darker, than any Mediterranean type, and just now quite clearly in a state of considerable emotional shock, for his lips and hands trembled and his dark brown eyes flickered from side to side, never resting on his interviewer for more than a second before darting away. From time to time he mopped his face with a clean white handkerchief that he pulled from the breast pocket of his neat black jacket.

"It is because we have been informed of your friendship with Miss Tan Sunee that we have asked you to come here," Robertson said. "You will have heard of her death, no doubt."

"Naturally," Ahmed repeated, but now in a whisper, adding, "On the radio. I have not been to the hospital for two days, because of illness."

"We have now got the postmortem report," Robertson told him. "Miss Tan Sunee was strangled two days ago."

Ahmed gave a low quavering moan and collapsed over the table before him.

Instant restoring treatment soon brought him round. An open and shut case the Detective Superintendent had already decided and this behaviour seemed to clinch it. But they must go through all the necessary motions extra carefully, so he helped his easy suspect to contact and employ a lawyer, also of his own race, to attend at once while the pharmacist made his statement and what turned out to be also his confession.

Ali Ahmed had indeed known Tan Sunee very well.

He had been conducting an affair with her, using for their meetings the store room on the second floor of the Isobel Saunders, and the inner store room of that place. Miss Tan always went there first, because it was she who got the key. He did not know how she got it.

"The other nurses, the ones who told me about your friendship with her, have explained that," Robertson told him.

A flash of anger passed from Ahmed to his lawyer, who shook his head and frowned, but did not speak.

Two days ago he had gone to the meeting place at about five in the afternoon. The door was open, as he expected it would be. He went in and passed on into the inner room. He thought she was asleep. He found—

"Go on!"

"She was *dead*! I collapsed. Then I went home. I was ill, very ill!"

"You killed her!"

"I did not! I did not! Why should I kill the girl I was in love with?"

"Why did you not at once raise the alarm in the hospital?"

"Too much afraid. This girl, from another country, not my religion, not my race. My position at the hospital."

"I think you had quarrelled with her. We have been given certain information."

"You may have been given lies," the lawyer suggested.

He had evidently not found much sympathy for his new client, quite unknown to him before that evening. He already had grave doubts about him. Besides, the police were behaving perfectly correctly. Here was an obvious suspect, a weak, frightened person, making an early confession that was as nearly complete as made no matter.

"I did not kill her! I did not kill her!" Ali insisted, upon a rising note. "I have told you the truth. I have not hidden my bad behaviour. I tell you I have found her."

"But you have not told the whole truth," Robertson insisted. "You were angry with her. You agree to that?"

Ali's mouth slackened; tears gathered in his large dark eyes.

"Allah knows I had good cause," he muttered.

His lawyer turned upon him.

"What are you saying now?" he demanded angrily. "You make more confession?"

"Those girls, her friends, they hate me, they speak against me!" The terrified pharmacist was almost beyond speech.

Detective Superintendent Robertson had had enough. He was not a vindictive man. He was experienced and fair, but without much imagination. He had Scottish forebears of a puritan cast of mind that led him into more than average racial prejudice. He realised that he had less than firm evidence of Ali Ahmed's guilt in respect of murder, but the man's confession was good enough to hold him for further interrogation without as yet making a charge.

He explained this to the two Pakistanis, both of whom seemed relieved that the questions had come to an end for the present. He made a point of escorting the lawyer to the door of the Station.

"I hope you will be able to attend again in the morning, sir," he said. "We should have confirmatory evidence by then from the spot where the body was found. Also a really complete list of every object found there, relevant and not relevant."

"You have mentioned other nursing staff. It was they who gave you my client's name, I understand?"

"Correct."

"He did not dispute this? Very unwise. But I think he is an honest person. Otherwise I would not continue with the case."

He shook hands very formally with the Detective Superintendent before getting into his car. Robertson stood gravely watching as he drove away.

The interview the next morning was brief and took the case no further. The strangled girl's finger nails provided, as they often did in such cases, some scraps of human skin, together with minute threads of material that might turn out to be part of the murderer's clothing or could well, in the circumstances, have already lain on the cushions of that sleazy love nest where she had been found, and picked up in her last feeble scrabbling attempt to breathe.

Still not good enough for a charge, Robertson decided, for the young man loudly, and after a night's rest with due appreciation of his position, the exchange of anxiety for desperation, with unexpected firmness, proclaimed again his moral turpitude but his innocence of murder.

So the detective went back to the hospital and to Sister Byrnes. There was a certain matter to be sorted out here, too.

Sister Mary Byrnes was looking positively ill this morning, Robertson noted. Her thin, intelligent face was pale with dark shadows below her eyes, her lips pale, too, indrawn except when she spoke, which she clearly found an effort.

He was concerned and showed it.

"You don't look fit for duty this morning, Sister," he said, kindly. "You've taken this thing very much to heart. Don't think I'm criticising. It does you credit."

Sister Byrnes laid her head on her small desk and burst into ragged sobs.

The Detective Superintendent, far from being embarrassed by this display of feeling, considered it a godsend and followed it up.

"I won't stay long," he said, disregarding the bent head and the continued flow of tears. "Just wanted to clear up the matter of the keys to the store room and who have the right to handle them."

Mopping her eyes and lifting a blotched face to him Sister said, "Basically, I do. But there are two duplicates and they all should hang on the board here above my desk. The nurses do occasionally ask for one, but very seldom. I have wondered sometimes if they have borrowed one simply to get it copied. They are quite ordinary Yale keys, as you see. But there is nothing of any value in the store room now. Only the rule is to keep the doors locked."

"You have never spoken to – what is she called now, Nursing Officer, is it? I mean about the keys and their purpose and the nurses perhaps having their own?"

"Never."

She spoke indignantly; her domain was under her control; not for guidance, control, possibly reprimand. Robertson retreated. Too soon for that approach. She could see criticism of herself ahead of it.

"But you did follow up any possible misuse of the keys, I suppose?"

"Of course."

"Yesterday, when I asked you in our first inquiries what was the last time you have gone to that room you said you could not remember, but it was several days. Whereas Miss Tupper, who discharged herself immediately after the discovery of the body, tells me she reported to you two days previously that she had found the door open and that you went along at once to lock it up again."

The change in Sister's face was startling, as much in its swift transformation from weak self-pity to fierce anger as in the small content of his news.

"Why does that upset you, Sister Byrnes? Did you in fact go to the store room after hearing from Miss Tupper that it was open?"

"Of course."

"What did you find there?"

"Nothing. What should I have found?"

Her recovery was as rapid as her swift rush of anger had been. She was back in her former role, the overworked nurse with subordinates she neither liked nor understood.

"That is for you to tell me. You said you had not been to the store for several days."

"Two days. Several days. I don't keep a diary in my head."

Her confidence had grown again as quickly as it had been shaken. But she added, unwisely, "I'm surprised you pay any attention to what that geriatric patient said to you. A prying person, poor old soul. Not quite – well, it's not for me to say. Unfortunately her treatment allowed her a very free range in the corridors. Mischief-making without meaning it, of course."

With a few more questions to establish the dates and times of Miss Tupper's admission, operation and follow-up treatment, Detective Superintendent Robertson took his leave of Sister, after warning her that he had further questions to put to her nurses. For this purpose he said he would have to see them separately. He had arranged for this with the Matron or whatever she was called now and would call them down to her office in pairs. He had laid on an interpreter.

Sister seemed to be indifferent to this development. Or perhaps she was stunned by it, regretting, but incapable of recalling, her stupid admission that the nurses disliked her and she them. She made no objection to Robertson's plan; how could she if he had Nursing Officer's permission. She did not even insist upon telling them that they had *her* permission to leave the ward in pairs.

Robertson went down to the ground floor to find his interpreter. This was a fairly recent recruit to the Police Force who had done his compulsory military service in the Far East when he was nineteen, following it by staying abroad to work in a British export firm, before returning to England to find fresh work where he could use his knowledge of several eastern languages. From the courts and various social and charitable bodies he had made contact several times with the police. If his command of the rarer immigrant tongues was less than perfect in some cases, at least his British fellow citizens could understand him. His name was Johnson, he was forty-five, solid but not fat, soft spoken, with a pleasant smile.

The Detective Superintendent collected Johnson and went back to the second floor. Here they moved together into the righthand ward, away from Sister's room. They walked slowly along, looking into all open doors, seeing a few old people in beds, but no nurses.

They found the staff, huddled together beside the telephones, chattering to one another in low voices. They did not look up at the noise of feet in the corridor. Only when Robertson said briskly "Which of you is the charge nurse here?" did they spring apart, one or two to their feet, the rest into an even closer crouching group, sitting on low stools.

"Go ahead," Robertson said to his companion.

Johnson greeted them. He knew their race; they spoke one of the languages he was most familiar with. But they did not respond at first. Not until he had conveyed the order Robertson had given, for two at a time to go to Matron's room downstairs, did one of them answer Robertson's question.

"I am charge nurse. We speak English here."

"Tell them to follow," Robertson said, turning away towards the stairs.

They gave in, but reluctantly. They tried to tell the Law nothing, but Johnson had quick ears and he knew far more than they imagined. At the end of it all the detective was able to confirm what Sister Byrnes had told him. They hated her, because she harried them over their work. They had been born and bred in a warm climate, they had no wish to work at all, but they liked money and there was plenty of it even if it had been found in this freezing land of great clumsy giants. Sister Byrnes hated them, and particularly Tan Sunee.

"Why so?"

"Because Tan Sunee wanted money, always money. Sister had to give it to her."

"Why so?"

They giggled and nudged one another, but they would not say.

"Blackmail?" suggested Johnson.

"I should think very unlikely. But possible, I suppose. Let's have the next pair."

"It will be the same all round, I'm afraid," Johnson foresaw.

And he was right. Every questioning led to the perpetual friction with Sister. This came first, then the bad morals of Tan Sunee. Then Sister's probable secret, belonging solely to Tan Sunee, not shared, a matter leading to giggles and then silence.

Silence, too, in every case, about Ali Ahmed. None of them would mention his name.

Back at the Station Detective Sergeant Craig said, "But I thought I heard you tell Miss Tupper, sir, that the nurses had named Ali and that was why we pulled him in."

"Actually it was the helper they call the 'tea lady'. She asked particularly not to be named. He needn't have spoken. Lost his nerve, I suppose."

"Looks like the names are piling up, sir."

"Looks like we can't believe a bloody one of them, as usual."

5

Aunt Amy continued to be by turns apologetic, by turns enthusiastically 'on the ball'. When Ali Ahmed was charged with murder, appeared before the magistrates and was remanded in custody to appear again, she shook her head and murmured, "Poor boy! Poor young man! His own fault. He behaved very stupidly, but not murder. Certainly not that."

"I don't see how you can be so sure," Phyllis told her. "Except I suppose the police have only got what they call circumstantial evidence."

"Which is the same as mine," Aunt Amy argued. "Only I actually saw the murderer and he saw that I recognised him. He was terrified. I am prepared to swear to that."

Phyllis could not offend her aunt by giving her Tom's view of the unknown hospital visitor's agitation. On the other hand the police, who probably agreed with him, were not prepared to lose sight of Miss Tupper, but had asked her to stay on with her relations for the present.

Aunt Amy had welcomed this request with pleasure. Sooner or later she would be vindicated. In the meantime she read and listened and watched all the usual sources of information, avidly, carefully even making notes and lists of events and persons involved in them.

Her delight was great, therefore, when Tom came home to announce that Michael Beddoes, the surgeon, had rung him up at his office in Newchester to ask if the Beddoes might meet and talk with Miss Tupper, who had been in the Isobel Saunders on the day of the murder of the nurse, but had left abruptly a few hours after the discovery of the crime.

"I hope you said yes," Aunt Amy cried, in some excitement. "I wonder what he wants."

"When did you ask him for?" Phyl said, not at all pleased.

"I suggested he and his wife might drop in for a drink any evening this week about six-thirty."

They all heard the door bell ring.

"That'll be them!" Aunt Amy clasped her hands in great excitement.

"Keen, aren't they?" Phyl muttered. "Aren't you going to let them in, darling? They're your guests."

The Beddoes quite understood that their appearance was too prompt, too soon after the polite, but cool invitation. It was Mrs. Beddoes, Molly, who had pointed this out to her surgeon husband.

"Mike, you really have a nerve! Poor chap, what else could he say? You make him scrape off lumps of your income tax, so he daren't lose his own fat little commission, so he knows he has to oblige you."

"Balls," Mike answered. "As far as I can get out of that copper in charge, Hunt's old aunt says she's seen the murderer. And it wasn't our little Ali. I've got to know exactly who it was she saw."

"I'm surprised that detective man—"

"Superintendent Robertson."

"Him. I'm surprised he told you about Mr Hunt's aunt at all."

"Actually he didn't. It was Sister Byrnes. But he agreed she did tell him."

"Sister Byrnes?"

"No. The aunt person, love."

"I still think we ought to leave it a day or two."

"I still think we'll go now."

So that was what they did and Molly knew that she had been right and Mike did not care and Aunt Amy jumped up as Tom showed them into the sitting room and went forward to be introduced.

Molly Beddoes began her prepared speech.

"I do apologise, Mrs. Hunt, for us barging in like this."

But no one paid any attention to her because Aunt Amy had said to Beddoes "You're one of the surgeons, aren't you? Not mine. Veins. Not your line, I expect. You want to know who it was I saw that day the girl was strangled and that poor boy is going to be blamed for it."

Michael Beddoes nodded.

"Yes, Miss Tupper. That's exactly what I want you to tell me. Because I know Ali Ahmed has practically landed himself a life sentence, but I'm perfectly sure he's right when he says he didn't do it."

Phyllis said, "Mrs. Beddoes – Molly, isn't it? Shall we push them off to Tom's study and then we can have a drink in comfort? I've heard Aunt Amy's story already, of course."

She did not add that another recitation of it would make her scream or vomit, but her expression led the visitors to understand that this would be the outcome.

"Good idea," Michael Beddoes said pleasantly.

"I'll show you," Tom agreed.

Aunt Amy went over, once again, a careful detailed account of the appearance and movements of the two men on the landing, their brief stop there, their exit in opposite directions, one down the main staircase, the other along the corridor of the other part of the ward. She described how she had concluded they had come out of the landing store room door, how she had found it unlocked and looked in. How the inner door was shut, but she had not tried it. How she had reported the state of the landing door to Sister before returning to her own room.

"Did you see Sister go to lock it up?"

"No. But I did notice as I left her office that she was reaching up to the board on the wall behind her desk where there are several keys hanging."

"She tells me she did go along and this was about four o'clock or just before. She saw nothing out of order, she says, but just looked in as you did and then locked the door and went back to her office."

"That would be before the Pakistani boy went there, wouldn't it?" Miss Tupper asked.

"Well, no. It couldn't have been. According to him, he wouldn't have been able to get in, would he? He has never had a key to that store room, neither the outer or the inner door."

"The papers say he had a date with the dead girl. She could get the keys duplicated for them both to have them. We don't know, do we? Unless Sister did not go to lock the door until much later than she says."

"She told me she went at once," Beddoes insisted. "It was locked, of course, when the other nurses went there and found the body. They had the regulation nurses' keys. All quite in order."

"Too much locking and unlocking!" Aunt Amy said, throwing up her hands in a very theatrical gesture.

"Too many visits to that store room all taking place over about an hour on one single afternoon," the surgeon said, adding thoughtfully, "We shall really want to know exactly how many people were in the hospital and whereabouts in it during that particular hour. Not easy."

"How on earth could you make a list like that? Would it be possible?"

"I doubt it, nowadays. There was a time, when porters were porters and didn't fancy themselves as little Hitlers. They considered their job then as helping people to find the right spot in the hospital where they would get treatment and their relations where to find them. And to keep out all undesirables. In my student days at my teaching hospital the porters were marvellous. They knew every face and every name that worked there. At the poor old Isobel Saunders now I doubt if Harris, the head porter, knows all his own lot; he'd feel insulted if you expected him to know how many people worked in the kitchens or even in the canteen where he goes for his meals."

"Then we can't find out or at least be sure of discovering who were workers and who were strangers that afternoon?"

"*We* can't. I mean not the Hunts or you or myself. But naturally the police will be doing their best and they have both ways and means."

"I suppose so. Less than they had, but they do manage to do marvels, all the same. I wish that plain clothes one, Robertson, would take my evidence seriously."

"You mean about seeing The Black Cat?" Michael was smiling indulgently. "He must be quite old now, Miss Tupper. White-haired, surely? Your chap was dark, wasn't he?"

"Black, of course," said Miss Tupper. "Dyed, if necessary."

It was possible, Beddoes considered, but most unlikely. Besides, the police probably knew all about the Cat's present whereabouts. They would have kept in touch with him. Two years since his discharge. Over sixty, he must be. Any health record? Might be able to get some information on that. Better not discuss the point with this eager old Aunt Amy.

"I will be seeing Ali in the near future, I hope," he said. "Or his lawyer. Probably both. Hadn't we better go back to the others?"

He offered a hand to Miss Tupper, who took it because he was a surgeon and she was feeling grateful to surgeons just then, even if he did seem to feel like treating her as a cripple.

"You are very confident in that young man's innocence," she said as they moved out of the study. "Why?"

He answered her briefly, for they needed only a few steps to reach the sitting room door. He stretched a hand to the knob.

"Yes," he said, holding the door open for her to pass in before him.

He offered no fuller explanation of his interest in the case, neither to Aunt Amy nor to his wife, Molly, as they drove away from the Hunts' house.

But he asked himself the same question when he lay in bed, unable to sleep, with Molly breathing gently and peacefully beside him. Why did he care about the

Asian pharmacist? The chap had confessed to having a sordid affair with one of the oriental nurses, hadn't he? On the hospital premises, too.

That wasn't like him. How did he know that? Because he had developed a liking for the lad. He was a worker and he had brains. He had come up with a very intelligent, extremely imaginative alteration in the chemo-therapy of one of his own patient's post-operative care. That showed an unusual interest in cases, in people, as well as in doses. It had made a much-needed advance possible. Michael remembered the modest way Ali had come to him with his suggestion, his own initial response, indignation, prejudice, prompting instant rejection. Then Ali's patient careful explanation which was too reasonable to be turned away without giving it a trial. Which had been followed by undeniable success.

So was this the kind of man to indulge in a dirty little hole-and-corner lay; to quarrel with the little tart, to squeeze the life out of her and leave her where she died?

No, he wasn't. Moreover more than once Ali had told him it was a mistake to have these girls as nurses. Dangerous. They did not understand drugs, not the drugs used as medicines, only the addictions, the aphrodisiacs, the cosmetics. Some day one of them would make a big mistake.

Then why had Ali started this affair? Surely he didn't need to. As a Moslem, with friends of his own persuasion, he would know how to provide himself with suitable women as and when he needed them? There must be more behind Ali's confession that he was still concealing. Beddoes was determined to force it out and in that resolution he found sleep at last.

The surgeon's time was never his own except during his statutory annual weeks of leave. So it was a few days before he was able to arrange to see the accused man's lawyer to explain his interest in the pharmacist and try to get permission to see him.

But the police, whose sole aim was to find some real evidence to support the charge of murder, were continuing their interviews with the hospital staff, fully aware that as time passed the stories they got would become fuller and less accurate.

All the same it did appear to be quite certain that the murder had caused no stir of deep emotion, no wild horror, no great anger; in fact no upset of any lasting kind. Tan Sunee had been working on the second floor ward on the morning of the day she must have died. She had not been seen by anyone after about three-thirty that afternoon. Those on duty with her had not been surprised by her absence. Tan Sunee kept hours of her own. All her little friends said so. Had they never reported her to Sister? One of them said she had done so. The rest said they had not. No reason given in either case.

Sister denied both the report and Nurse Tan's default. The reporting nurse, questioned again, said that Sister was afraid of Tan Sunee and also hated her. Why? With a bent head and sidelong glance of small black eyes the nurse spoke about money. Tan Sunee loved money. She had come to England for no other reason than to make money. To her any and every method was right if it was successful. She had often been successful.

The implication was obvious. The victim had been a blackmailer and doing well, already very experienced. Put to her directly by the interpreter, the nurse agreed.

"But to blackmail Sister? What possible hold could she have?" Robertson wanted to know.

The nurse shook her head. She had not been a friend of the dead girl. They must ask her friends, those three who had found her body, when her absence had begun to be noticed widely, not only by the nurses on the second floor.

"Had Sister Byrnes not noticed it or asked about it?"

"She would not do so. She was afraid of her and hated her."

Round to the beginning again. Another session with Sister Byrnes. And no progress whatever, only a further depressing picture of the difficulties, even perils of managing the Isobel Saunders Hospital with a mixed staff, whose ways of thought and principles of conduct belonged to several widely different beliefs and customs, some alien, some native to Britain.

Sister's twisted smile of rejection did not help Robertson when he told her of the nurse's account of Tan Sunee's cupidity.

"We all knew we couldn't trust that one," she said.

"You did not tell me that before."

"I didn't want to speak ill of her. She had paid for it, hadn't she?"

"Certainly." Robertson raised his voice. "And I intend to find the villain responsible."

He reddened. What a way to speak. Tele crime serial stuff. He felt ashamed.

But Sister Byrnes was looking at him coldly; it would be useless to ask her straight out if she had been blackmailed. She was well on her guard. Besides, there was another matter of more importance in which she might help.

"How many keys are there to that store room?" he asked, as abruptly as she had agreed to the dead girl's bad behaviour.

Sister glanced round at the key board behind her on the wall and considered.

"For this floor I keep one here on the board and a spare in my desk drawer now," she said. "I know the nurses have one of their own, but I have never managed to see it and they always deny it isn't the official one that they are allowed."

"You mean you know they have two?"

"Yes. Then there must be one in the admin. department, what used to be the Secretary's office. Anyone doing a repair job on this ward, the engineers and so on, keep their tools in the store room, or use it for mending things, putting parts together, that sort of thing. But there wasn't any work being done here on that afternoon. Not that I was told about."

"No. We've been into that. There wasn't," Robertson told her.

Later that day in his office at the Police Station he found Detective Sergeant Craig waiting for him.

"Well?" he asked.

"I went back to the works department at the hospital and checked again on any work done the day of the murder, as before. No job of importance anywhere. A few small repairs in situ and a few undertakings started in the hospital workshops. Then I made special inquiry as you suggested, sir, about keys being taken and returned when they have to go anywhere usually kept locked up. It was a girl in charge, girl clerk type of bint, easy on the eye, agreeable—"

"Never mind her appearance," Robertson interrupted. "What could she tell you about the store room key?"

"That it had been borrowed by the firm of builders who have recently been given an extension job of some sort."

"Who borrowed it? Which firm? Local?"

"Newchester firm. The girl didn't know the man who called for the key. But he came in with their own Mr. Crawthorne, who is the hospital architect."

"Give me the yellow pages," Robertson ordered.

The Newchester Builders had a good-sized advertisement in the section of the telephone directory relating to their business. It described the wide range of the firm's capability and achievement, including public works.

A call to the main offices of the Newchester Builders brought Robertson in touch with the secretary to the managing director. She agreed that the firm was concerned with a project at the Isobel Saunders Hospital. Yes, the head of the firm had been at the hospital several times together with the architect. Yes, she was sure he would be willing to see Detective Superintendent Robertson.

The latter put back the receiver with a grim face.

"The character from the builders who had the keys to the store room that afternoon was the head of the firm," he told Craig. "You may be interested to know his name is Tilsett."

"Blimey!" Craig struck the table between them. "What price the old girl now? Second sight or what?"

6

The Detective Superintendent was not impressed, or not outwardly. He found Detective Sergeant Craig rather a trial, though his frivolous remarks were not as utterly pointless as those of some other of his colleagues. Also the Sergeant was quite serious in following up any arrangement; very painstaking, very dogged.

"Tilsett isn't an uncommon name hereabouts," he said. "We know this builder chap, managing director, his office calls him head of the firm. He isn't that villain they let out a couple of years ago. The odds are he isn't a relation either. And longer still that he and the other fellow had anything to do with this murder. But you can have the pleasure of finding me right or wrong, Sergeant. Check with Tilsett that he and the hospital architect, Crawthorne, did visit the Isobel Saunders on the date given by our Pakistani suspect. The same date old Miss Tupper and Sister Byrnes looked into the store room, or so they all say."

"Only Miss Tupper says she saw the two men and identified—"

"Never mind that. You get them squared off and find out if either or both saw Miss Tupper, staring at them and jigging up and down. Marking time she calls it; part of her post-op varicose vein treatment."

Sergeant Craig suppressed a laugh.

"Ask Tilsett why he left the door unlocked and what he did with the key. Ask him if he is connected in any way with our ex-convict Tilsett. Find out if he has any form himself and check that. O.K.?"

"Yes, sir."

While Detective Sergeant Craig set about his inquiries, beginning at the hospital with a further search in the works department to re-check the date of the Newchester Builders' latest visit, Detective Superintendent Robertson demanded and was granted an interview with the Area Administrator of the National Health Service.

Mr. Philip Newbury had been housed at great expense in part of a new office block in Newchester, originally intended as much-needed housing for an inflated list of local homeless. To build the block a row of pleasant Georgian houses, neglected, but with solid walls though no modern facilities inside, had been demolished. When the block, after three years of intermittent wrangling and construction, was nearly finished, it was found that it could not be filled because no one on the housing list would consent to live above the second storey. They had heard too much about shaky balconies and sabotaged lifts. So the housing scheme had to be abandoned and the upper storeys advertised as office space, while a few families were placed on the lower floors.

But even this did not succeed, because no one would take offices above two storeys of harassed mums and screaming children and lift vandals.

Instead some rather inferior, delapidated and shabby but sound Victorian large houses were taken over for conversion into flats and the new tower block was equipped for Mr. Newbury and his troop of assistant administrators. This occupied the whole of the ground and first floors. The second floor housed the warehouse of a sports equipment firm and that above the premises of a new weekly magazine.

Robertson was not kept waiting. He was unexpectedly welcome. Where the hospital consultants, senior and junior, and housemen, had been grim and apart from the surgeon, Beddoes, had stiffened the upper lip and murmured their disapproval of foreign staff in general, the Area Administrator's office was seething with sentimental emotion, shock, embarrassment, horror at violent death in a place of healing, a frantic search for an adequate scapegoat.

"This is very good of you, Superintendent," Mr. Newbury said, springing to his feet as Robertson was shown in by a handsome dark girl, who shut the door behind him, excluding herself at the same time. "Come and sit down. Can I get you—?"

"No thanks," the officer said, but he accepted the seat offered him, deciding to watch the administrator clearing his own department of any possible blame before he himself stated the question he had come to have answered.

"You will understand our concern over this matter," Mr. Newbury went on, sitting down again but leaning forward over his desk. "Terrible concern. Great responsibility, these foreign girls, you understand. Different standards, different life style."

"In this case," Robertson interrupted, "the killing seems to have been no different from half a dozen done by our own people over the last couple of months."

Mr. Newbury swallowed nervously.

"The murderer was also one of our Health Service employees, but not of the same race," he said. "Am I right?"

"We have a Pakistani who has been remanded in custody," Robertson told him. "He asked the magistrates' court to lift press restrictions, because he insists upon giving certain evidence about seeing, but not reporting at once, the body of the dead girl."

"I have read all that in the papers," Newbury said in a disappointed voice.

"Yes, sir."

As the administrator made no further attempt to drag inside information from Robertson the latter began to explain the reason for his call.

"We are trying to find and speak to all visitors to the hospital on the day it has been established the nurse was killed," he begun. "This has been particularly difficult since the body was not found for two days, nor did the girl's disappearance cause any alarm during that time. Her companions knew that she did not always report for duty. Sometimes they gave her name as well as their own. It was not checked. The Sister in the ward says these girls are very much alike to look at—"

"That is absurd," said Mr. Newbury angrily. "A well worn, a worn-out prejudice! Ridiculous, if it wasn't racially serious."

"We know we have not traced, possibly never will trace, all the outside visitors during those two days, but are concentrating on any who may have gone to the second floor on business and of those any who had a possible purpose in going into the store room there. They would need the key of that door, which was normally kept locked."

It was clear that the Area Administrator had no idea at all of the geography of the Isobel Saunders. He looked bewildered but making an effort said, "What did you find?"

"We found that the hospital architect, a Mr. Crawthorne, with the managing director of a construction firm called Newchester Builders, a Mr. Tilsett, had indeed been there on that date. Mr. Tilsett had borrowed the key for the store room on the second floor and had returned the key to the works department later the same afternoon. I would like to know if you can tell me any reason why these two men were there. Were they engaged on any project connected with the hospital?"

Mr. Newbury stared. The vaguely amiable expression left his face and his small features set hard and did not relax as he answered, after a few seconds pause, "Why yes, of course," and stopped again as he pressed a small button on his desk.

The girl who had shown Robertson in appeared again and was given a brief order.

"I'll show you," Mr. Newbury said. "There is a project for the Isobel Saunders. New operating theatres on the second floor. Passed at the last Regional meeting, awarding the job to Newchester Builders."

"So the architect and Tilsett had a perfectly valid reason for being there, on the second floor, that day?"

"Certainly they had."

"The project had already been considered?"

"It had already been awarded to Newchester Builders."

Still staring in his former manner from a fixed face Newbury added, "They are a reliable firm; they have worked for the Health Service before. Not a large firm, but reliable."

And if I want any more dope on Tilsett I can go dig for it myself, Robertson thought, as he got up to go.

"Just one more point, sir," he said, "about Mr. Crawthorne. Does he work locally? Private practice as well, or only for the Health Service?"

"For the Service, but the whole region," Mr. Newbury answered. "Appointed by the Regional Administrator."

"And that is?"

"Sir Frank Pelman."

"Yes, of course, I ought to have remembered. Thank you, sir, very much for your collaboration."

Mr. Newbury attempted a smile but it appeared more like a grin though there was rather an odd gleam in his deepset eyes to go with it, Robertson decided. Never mind. There need not be any mystery over those two specialists' presence on the second floor landing when Miss Tupper had come upon them. Only one more thing was needed in that respect. That Miss Tupper should identify the pair in person.

"Well, I don't know so much about that," Aunt Amy said briskly, when the Detective Superintendent put it to her. "I've already told you he parted from the other one and walked off with his back to me. Besides, it was the face of the one nearest to me who turned and stared and I was petrified and so was he. He turned and ran—"

"Downstairs, I know." The Superintendent realised from experience that Miss Tupper's story had set in its final form, stiffer than frozen food, more like the grouting powder with which he had recently fixed some new tiles in his bathroom at home.

"But the figure you saw marching away," he went on. "What was it like?"

"Not as tall as the other. Stockier. Wide shoulders. Hair thin on top at the back; you could see the crown through. Why does this always happen to me, but hardly ever—"

"Do you think you would recognise that back?" Robertson was not to be diverted.

"I might. I would know the other one, though. So ought you," she added unexpectedly.

"That other one is the regional architect for this district as part of that area. His name is Victor Crawthorne and he has held the post for five years. He is thirty-four, unmarried, lost his parents in childhood. Can I persuade you that he is *not* the released murderer, Tilsett?"

Miss Tupper was surprised, but not noticeably downcast.

"Well, all I can say," she spoke crisply after a short interval, "is that he must be a close relative or else it's one of those unlikely coincidences."

"You don't think your own memory might possibly be at fault?"

"No, I don't. I checked my newspaper files as soon as my niece could find them for me."

"You have them here?"

"Of course. I'll get them for you."

Robertson could not deny that the general appearance of the convicted criminal, both in the photofit attempt to portray him and his real likeness after arrest did bear a certain resemblance to young Crawthorne, who had confirmed his visit with the building manager, Tilsett, on the afternoon in question. But then, as he pointed out to Miss Tupper, narrow-faced dark men with thick eyebrows were not an uncommon type. One could expect to see several in any crowd or queue.

"But not glaring like wild beasts," said Aunt Amy firmly, "like the man I saw on the landing."

Which brought the conversation to an end but made the Detective Superintendent more determined than ever to confront Miss Tupper with the two men who had already confirmed they were the pair she described.

Each had explained the purpose of the joint visit. They had discussed the details of the alterations to be made on the second floor. Their tour of the area had included a visit to the store room. The site it occupied would be used in the extended plumbing needed for the modern theatre unit. They had wanted to confirm that it was not in use for the ward as it was at the moment.

"Did you find the store room was in any sort of use?" Robertson asked.

"None." Mr. Tilsett was most emphatic.

"The small inner room or cupboard also? You found nothing unusual there?"

"I did not look inside. I don't recollect Victor looking in either."

Which really proved nothing of course. In fact Tilsett, who offered all possible help from the moment his visit had been confirmed at the works department, had suggested one thing only and that without meaning to. He had shown that keys to any locked feature in the hospital were available on demand, without any sort of notification, neither time nor signature of the borrower, merely the date of the borrowing and that of return of the key or keys. All very casual, slap-happy and no bloody help to further his case one way or another, Robertson decided.

But he was still anxious to confront Miss Tupper herself with the only two men he had discovered who could fit her crazy description. While he continued to search for real evidence of Ali Ahmed's guilt, he must at least wipe the board clean of other suspects. If you could call those Englishmen suspects, which he was very reluctant to do, especially in such a way as to prevent them suspecting his ulterior motive.

He did manage it however by taking Miss Tupper into his confidence. She had told him she was due to visit the Isobel Saunders again to see her surgeon. He had not been able to fix the time with Mr. Tilsett of his visit to the hospital with the architect, he told her. Neither the builder nor Mr. Crawthorne could pinpoint it exactly, he said. So would she go with him to the hospital works department, before her appointment with her surgeon, meet the two gentlemen and discuss that time with them. It was very important because the man at present charged with the murder was not sure of the exact time at which he had discovered the nurse, dead.

Miss Tupper was delighted. Not only did she realise that the detective was taking her seriously at last, but here was an opportunity for real drama of the most exciting kind. She agreed to Detective Superintendent Robertson's plan with enthusiasm.

She found the result dampening, to say the least of it. Mr. Tilsett, the builder, bore no slightest resemblance to the notorious criminal of that name. But nor did the architect, his colleague. Mr. Tilsett was clearly middle-aged, but by no means in his sixties. His hair was thinning, as she had observed from his back view, and was uniformly grey. His face, which she was now seeing for the first time, was red, round, with features sunk into the surrounding fat and with no marked expression. He listened to her emphatic declaration of the time of their encounter and was ready to confirm it without question.

Not so his companion, the architect, in whose hospital workshop office the meeting took place. Mr. Crawthorne was a young man, in his early thirties, Aunt Amy decided. He was dark, his curly hair rather too long and unruly, with sideburns that gave him a bushy appearance. Though not exactly handsome he had an alert intelligent look and a very pleasant smile.

He had listened to Miss Tupper's explanation of her presence at the end of the ward and the reason for her certainty about the exact time she had been there.

"I remember you," he said. "I remember distinctly. You were standing behind the glass door, but moving—"

"Marking time," said Aunt Amy. "You must have thought I was crackers—"

"Well—"

"You must have. Unavoidable. Ridiculous." Robertson intervened.

"You recognise one another, then?"

They agreed.

"You agree now over the time, sir?"

Crawthorne nodded, glancing sideways at Tilsett, who also nodded. The object of the exercise seemed to have been achieved.

Outside the hospital Robertson said, "There was no real difficulty over the time of your seeing those two, was there, Miss Tupper?"

"No."

"I hope you are convinced now that your fears over Mr. Tilsett were unfounded."

She hesitated.

"Oh, this Mr. Tilsett, yes. Nothing like. It isn't an uncommon name in these parts, I understand. But the young one, Crawthorne. Of course he looked different; he was trying to be as pleasant as possible. And succeeding. Quite attractive, actually, I thought. But I couldn't very well tell him to his face that he had a very different expression the first time I saw him. Wild, fierce, furiously angry, desperate – Well, I don't know how to describe it except to say those photos of the Cat came into my mind at once and I was terrified."

Detective Superintendent Robertson groaned inwardly. These obstinate old women. Still on about The Cat in spite of having it proved to her those two chaps were harmlessly at their jobs for renovating the hospital operating theatre system.

Miss Tupper went on to her appointment with her surgeon and came from that encouraged to continue her varied rest and exercise at home, if she preferred. Then she returned to the Hunts' house still puzzling over the two men she had met earlier.

Particularly the young one. Could those bold looks, that attractive smile, really be exchanged for the savage rage that had so terrified her? Was it really the same man on this occasion as on that?

Another thought struck her. If the two faces were so dissimilar, why was she so sure it was indeed the same man? And now she knew the answer. She had seen the good-looker before, in another photograph, a recent one, too.

Desperately she tried to remember where. It must

have been a newspaper, or why should she have thought of The Cat?

She rang up Robertson.

"Yes, I must have been mistaken," she confirmed at the end of her explanation. "I think a newspaper picture, but I'm not a hundred per cent sure on that point. The same Mr. Crawthorne as we saw today. Full face, looking quite calm, rather amused."

"In a newspaper?"

"I'm not sure."

"We'll check, Miss Tupper. You're sure your identification with the criminal was a mistake?"

"My shock, my horror, was no mistake, Mr. Robertson."

Detective Sergeant Craig could find no trace of any photograph of the architect in the local press of the last three months.

7

Gerald Nubb was one of the more recently elected town councillors serving the committees responsible for Newchester's health and social services, as well as its children's education. He was young for a bureaucrat supposed to be sufficiently experienced to serve on such important committees. He was in his middle forties, about the same age as Michael Beddoes. Together with his wife and one son he lived two houses away from the surgeon on the same side of the road.

Michael was having trouble at the hospital. There was a continuous flow of rumours there following the discovery of the strangled nurse; there were threats of a walk-out from her compatriot nurses and threats of strike action by porters, who complained that they were being harassed and bullied by the police, when, as Michael understood it, they were expected to do their job of monitoring people entering and leaving the building. In addition to all this the place still swarmed with journalists, popping out of all sorts of unlikely and forbidden rooms to interrupt his work and demand facts he had no intention of giving them even if he knew the answers to their silly questions. If only the hospital governors would make a final statement—

"Why don't you ask Gerald?" Molly suggested,

after several days of repeated moaning by her husband.

"Gerald? Which Gerald?"

"Nubb, of course. The councillor, isn't he? You always answer his questions about the garden. He owes you a few answers about the Isobel Saunders. Why they're holding up the start of the new theatres, for instance. Isn't that your chief worry at the moment?"

Michael nodded.

"You're quite right, as usual, darling. He's supposed to be rather bright in committee. Takes an interest anyway; not only in getting travel money to the county town. I hardly know him, though."

"Show him the new hedge-cutter. He was slaving away with some blunt shears yesterday afternoon."

Michael had no difficulty with this approach, for the councillor arrived at his gate very soon after the high-pitched whine of his own electric machine filled their immediate neighbourhood with hideous noise.

Mr. Nubb's admiring face appeared on the far side of Michael's level cut. He spoke, but the cutter drowned his words, so Michael switched it off.

"I do beg your pardon for disturbing you, Mr. Beddoes," the councillor said, with very formal politeness, "but I wonder if you would give me some information about that, er, utensil. I find difficulty these days – shears – always blunt."

"Come in," Michael interrupted the embarrassed flow. "I'll show you. A bit hard on the wrist. My wife won't use it. Afraid of electrocuting herself, I think. But it does the job very easily."

He held out his machine to Mr. Nubb who was now standing beside him.

"No, no. You show me. I might do it an injury." He laughed nervously.

By the time the front hedge was finished and the councillor had tried his hand at cutting it and had succeeded better than his retiring modesty had promised, Michael was able to invite him to come into the house and find the brochure, originally packed with the cutter, for Nubb to take away.

Molly, with drinks, stayed the councillor's departure. By the time he finally went he was promising they would hear the noise of another hedge being cut near them in a very few days. He would be due in the county town tomorrow at a meeting; he could buy the implement then.

"Business that will interest you, Mr. Beddoes," he said. "The project at the Isobel Saunders Hospital."

Unexpectedly rapid progress, Michael thought, avoiding Molly's eye.

"Our operating theatres? At last?" he asked, hoping he had judged the right note of excitement.

"Well, after the tragedy there recently. You understand."

"Of course."

"More than enough publicity. We cancelled one meeting. Besides there was trouble with staff, I understand."

"No staff ever takes criticism these days. Particularly if the police imply it."

"But I understand it was an obvious case. A foreigner, an immigrant—"

"No, Mr. Nubb," Molly said firmly. "There are foreign staff there, but they aren't immigrants."

"The nurses have trained in this country," Michael explained. "They are getting experience to take home, most of them. Ali Ahmed was a student here for several years before qualifying as a pharmacist. He is assistant pharmacist at the Isobel Saunders."

"Was, I think," said Mr. Nubb, stiffening under the opposition he found in both his hosts. "Suspended by Mr. Newbury, surely until – well, one must not pass judgment before the trial."

"He has not yet been sent for trial," Michael reminded him. "Only remanded in custody for a week. Not up till the day after tomorrow."

Mr. Nubb looked bewildered, but obstinate.

"But it *is* fairly obvious, isn't it?"

"It is not obvious at all." Michael was emphatic.

The councillor got up to go. He seemed to have dropped the case of Tan Sunee down a very dark but handy well. He thanked them both for their help, for the details of the cutter, for the sherry. He said they must return the visit and meet his wife. He set off back up the road at his usual slowish pace with his usual calm features unmoving.

"That is what is known as a solid citizen," Michael remarked, coming back from the gate into the house.

"Aren't you going to finish the hedge?"

"Bugger the hedge! That man has made up his mind Ali is guilty without knowing the first thing about it!"

"I was afraid you might put him off us. Let's hope you haven't."

"Yes, you may be right. I'll cultivate him carefully in future. He did mention Newbury after all."

"Who is Newbury?"

"The Health Service Area Administrator. Salary as long as his title and arrogance to match, for a jumped-up sort of clerical civil service type."

"Don't we call that bureaucrat and then spit?" Molly asked, gathering the glasses. "You finish the hedge and I'll finish getting dinner."

Though Mr. Nubb had given the Beddoes a distressingly biased opinion of the accused pharmacist's guilt, he had not really made up his mind about him. He was a fair-minded man, well able to sift evidence on most of the matters the council dealt with. Also his position on the committee that dealt with local public health business brought him in touch with officials of the National Health Service, including the Isobel Saunders. As a smallish hospital and in many ways old-fashioned, it was already threatened with closure in the not far distant future. This would be a terrible blow to Newchester, not only in the matter of convenience for local doctors and above all for their patients, but for local employment. The hospital provided a good measure of maintenance work in various trades, particularly for the plumbing, electrical and building sections. It was over this side of the affairs of the Isobel Saunders that Mr. Nubb was perplexed and anxious, rather than over the violent crime that had suddenly thrown the hospital and its small, unremarkable town upon the news media to the council's great shame and dismay.

For some time in the last year Mr. Nubb had been hearing things that disturbed him. Unexpected, unnatural things, happenings to his fellow councillors, a new car where the old one was in good order, a holiday in Greece when the Spanish beaches had been the rule for several years, innocent enough, surely, until one of them suggested he would get a bargain for the repainting of his garden fence if he used the Newchester Builders.

"Never heard of them," he had told the other councillor.

"*Surely?* Been putting in for some of our jobs. Very up and coming these last few months."

"I'd consider that a reason against using them, not for doing so," he had said severely and heard no more of it.

But the conversation came back to his mind when he heard that the Newchester Builders had landed the big contract for turning the second floor of the hospital from a minor orthopaedic and geriatric surgical ward into a highly modern surgical unit of two theatres with an intensive care ward accompanying them.

He wondered, and from wondering began to ask questions. Very discreet questions, very carefully put. Some of the answers were disturbing. He had a friendly interview with Philip Newbury, but got no help from it whatever. He did learn, however, from the council records, that the managing director of the Newchester Builders was called Raymond Tilsett.

Mr. Nubb was in his forties and had a very clear memory of the Black Cat murders. He had lived in or near Newchester all his life, so the name Tilsett did not alarm or even startle him as it had done Miss Tupper. There were several Tilsett families in the near neighbourhood, quite unconnected with crime. But he thought it might be interesting to know if there was any connection here, not, from his point of view, in any way with this nasty murder of a foreign nurse, but with his definite suspicion of bribery on the part of the builder.

In his quiet, efficient, self-effacing way, Mr. Nubb set to work to appease his conscience by cleaning up his Council.

Michael Beddoes, meanwhile, had been more impressed by the Hunts' Aunt Amy than he had allowed them to know. She was ridiculous of course, as one might expect from a retired actress, never of the top rank. But she was no fool; that was equally plain. She had jumped to an absurd conclusion, an impossible one, but she was not inventing the impression the two men on the landing had made upon her. Or rather the impression one of them had made. That had given her a real fright; she would not forget it. She had informed the police, Tom Hunt had said. They no doubt had been able to identify the pair. If he could do the same, he might be able to suggest a line of defence to Ali Ahmed's lawyer, who must be wondering by now whether he felt able to continue with the case.

Michael opened the subject with his registrar, Donald McRae, the next morning as they sat drinking coffee after an early operating session. McRae said he honestly hadn't given the thing much thought. Wasn't it a pretty sordid affair, but only to be expected. These little Far East dolly birds were hot numbers in some cases. He kept away, personally.

"Did you know Ali Ahmed was mixed up with Tan Sunee?"

"Yes, I knew."

"How?"

"I wanted some blood in a hurry. I expected to have to get it myself, but Ahmed was still around, after seven. He got me what I wanted and then joined me at the lift. I was surprised and asked him if he wasn't going home. He said not just yet."

"That doesn't mean anything."

"I know. That's why I asked around a bit. Paul told me about the second floor nurses. I wasn't interested."

Michael stared at him. Don had never struck him as being a strict puritan; a Scot, but not a Calvinist, not as strait-laced as he was just now trying to make himself out to be. But he said no more. Paul Waters, the houseman in his wards, would be likely to help him – perhaps.

Paul reluctantly did so, but on condition that none of it was passed on to the police. Tan Sunee had gone in for boy-friends in a big way and not only east of Suez.

"And Ali Ahmed was one of them?"

"The drugs mixer? Oh yes, he was one."

"Other staff?"

"Non-medical? Well, probably. But he could say he was on the job and leave it at that."

"Who was it, Paul? I'm asking for my own satisfaction. I won't hand it on. Anyway, the Law is sure to have got it already."

"Crawthorne, the architect. Occasionally with the builder chap. Very often alone."

Seeing the satisfaction on his chief's face he grew alarmed.

"But I never actually saw him with Tan Sunee. You won't quote me, sir, will you?"

"No, Paul. You go on looking after my patients and ignore the whole rotten business."

As I had better do myself, he decided. But he did report his finds to Tom Hunt that evening, though not their source.

"Seems our strangled victim ran quite a little brothel on the second floor," he told him. "Not that that is going to help poor Ali. It only suggests the jealousy motive, doesn't it?"

"It seems to me," Tom said, "from the mathematical point of view it is a point in his favour.

Two points, perhaps. Miss Tupper's two men, together, remember, on the landing. At just about the right time or a little before or after the girl's death. Is it supposed Crawthorne had just been having the girl with the builder looking on, or sharing, and then knocking her off at some point in the process?"

"If they did," said Beddoes, slowly, "surely they wouldn't have left that door unlocked, as they did. Miss Tupper may be haywire, but she does pin-point that vital time factor."

"Too right," Tom agreed gloomily.

Detective Superintendent Robertson was disappointed. Spurred on by Aunt Amy's continuing obstinacy, but unwilling to allow her any sort of victory in her ridiculous identification, he had gone to the archives of the local newspapers to look up both the text and the pictures of the crimes, arrest and trial of that notorious murderer, the so-called Black Cat. The police files on the subject he now knew by heart, as did Detective Sergeant Craig.

But the result of his new search was meagre. Reproductions of the photofit put out by themselves, in the early hunt for the killer, later police photos of the actual criminal and views of him being taken in and out of court with his head in a blanket. No bloody good, Robertson thought peevishly. He decided to wait until Miss Tupper went home to her own house, then call on her and ask to see the full range of her collection. Those her niece had fetched for him to see were the same as those he had gone through himself. But there had been more. He must really study the whole collection. From the way she described them they showed old Tilsett far more dramatically than anything he had found in Newchester.

In the meantime he continued to check on those two visitors to the hospital. The builder, Ray Tilsett, came of a local artisan family that had no known connection with the criminal. Ray himself was not altogether unknown to the police, as Craig had discovered, in the records of juvenile court appearances. He had stolen fruit and damaged the coping of an old garden wall to get at it. Later he had once had his licence endorsed for dangerous driving. But he bore no known relationship to the Black Cat. His life history had been gone into very thoroughly at the time of his first tangle with the Law, when he had narrowly escaped Borstal training. But that had been before the Black Cat had appeared on the scene.

As for Victor Crawthorne, he had come to Newchester when he had been appointed architect to the area hospitals as part of the National Health Service. He had been brought up by his grandparents after the death of his mother. His father was said to have died when he was a baby. He was unmarried. There was a vague, joking rumour among the hospital porters that young Crawthorne fancied the foreign nurses, but the rumour had no substance.

And yet, and yet, it was this very man, professional, hardworking, with a blameless, unfortunate childhood, deprived when young of both parents, who had given Miss Tupper such a fright, a severe, totally unexpected shock that happened at about the time of a brutal murder.

Was this pure chance or had it real meaning? Was it the result of an over-excited imagination, always given to exaggerate, or did Miss Tupper possess second sight, as it used to be called?

Robertson put aside these useless speculations and took up the newly-arrived, detailed pathological report of the postmortem on Tan Sunee, whose inquest had produced the expected verdict of 'Murder by person or persons unknown'.

8

Michael Beddoes followed the prison officer to the door of the pharmacist's cell, where they both halted. The officer slid aside the small viewing panel.

"Take a look, sir," he said in a low voice. "We're getting worried about this man. Won't speak at all now, except to his lawyer. Doesn't eat enough to keep a bird alive."

"But still insists he didn't strangle the nurse," Michael said, applying his eye to the opening.

Ali was sitting on the side of his narrow bed, upright, stiff, motionless, staring straight in front of him. His features were set in an expression of stark despair, utter hopelessness. It shocked Michael more than any wild, frantic fear or a fury of denial. Clearly something must be done to help the man and that quickly or he would not survive, at least his mind would not survive, to stand trial.

He turned to the prison officer.

"Is the lawyer here? I understood I was to see Mr. Ahmed in the presence of his lawyer."

"Yes, sir. Mr. Zimballah is already in the building. He will be here in a minute. He has been told you have arrived. We wanted you to take a look at the prisoner, quietly, first. Being a doctor, sir."

"I understand."

Mr. Zimballah, in charge of another officer, now appeared, and after Beddoes had been introduced to him the two men were allowed into the cell with the usual clicking of locks, but without the creaking and clanging of dungeon doors found necessary in radio presentations of such scenes.

The lawyer went in first. Ali Ahmed rose politely, but when he saw Michael's head behind and above Mr. Zimballah's shining black hair he gave a sharp cry, covered his face with his hands and collapsed again on to the bed.

Michael said quickly, "Ali, pull yourself together! I'm prepared to believe you didn't kill this girl. I know you better than Mr.—"

"Zimballah," the lawyer prompted.

"Mr. Zimballah. You have my backing but is it worth anything? How can Mr. Zimballah get up anything like a defence for you, unless you tell us much more about your connection with this girl."

"You despise me! You wish to relieve the hospital of this stain of a sordid death. You wish—"

"Rubbish!" said Michael furiously. "Stop the melodrama for God's sake! Nobody's despising you except your damned silly self!"

"And the newspapers!"

"Stuff the newspapers! Look, Ali. I'm a busy man, as you know perfectly well. You helped me not so long ago over the medication of a particularly tricky post-operative complication. I want to help you. I've been asking round at the Isobel Saunders about those little nurses on the second floor and I've got some interesting news. Apart from the patients and the other nursing staff, not Tan Sunee's little bunch, there were certainly two other unusual visitors on the afternoon you were booked to go there. So you can't be the only suspect, though admittedly at present you seem to be a likely one."

Ali Ahmed, who had been looking more alive, even interested, showed an inclination to collapse once more.

"Don't look like a stranded fish," Michael told him. "Just give us some reasonable explanation of what possessed you to take up with the girl. She was not of your race or religion or have you become so far westernised you no longer care about such things?"

He spoke harshly on purpose. He felt he must rouse a sense of outrage before he could hope for real confession.

He succeeded, but not quite in the way he had looked for. Ali's dark eyes brightened with genuine anger, his mouth twisted in self-hatred as he cried, "I had learned she was, could be had, and that the price was not so much as in the houses I know of, serving my own people, but expensive, you know."

"O.K. I don't blame you. I am not shocked. Nor is Mr. Zimballah, I think."

The lawyer shook his head, but he did not regard his client with any sort of indulgence.

"So what went wrong?" Michael asked.

"She wanted more than we agreed. Much more. When I refused she threatened to tell the authority I had forced her. It was blackmail. It was to go on and at her price. I was trapped."

"So to end it—"

"No! No, I did not kill her! I did not know how to end it. I thought I must break my contract and lose my permit."

"I must ask you," said Mr. Zimballah, speaking to Ali for the first time. "How did you pay this girl?"

"In cash. British currency. Always."

"And you kept a record of these payments?"

"No written record."

Mr. Zimballah shook his head.

"You make it impossible for me to make a defence."

Ali dropped his face into his hands again. His shoulders heaved as he began to sob.

Michael Beddoes was exasperated. The lawyer, never clearly enthusiastic for his countryman's rescue, was about to give up the attempt. If he did so the pharmacist's future was bleak. No British jury could possibly do other than find the man guilty on such clear circumstantial evidence. And yet – and yet – he still had that strong feeling deep in himself that the man whose sharp mind and active concern for a patient's dilemma had helped so very materially in that patient's recovery, could not allow himself to sink to a sordid and brutal solution of a money difficulty. Surely there was a hitch somewhere in this claim of evidence. The locked door? The time?

"Ali," he said, again brisk, commanding, "Pull yourself together, man! You swear your innocence. I want to believe you. Mr. Zimballah here isn't sure if he can." He raised an eyebrow at the lawyer, who only stared back at him, still totally unwilling to commit himself, one way or the other.

"Mr. Zimballah doesn't share my feeling," Beddoes went on. "So you've got to help yourself. First of all, do you know how Tan Sunee got into the store room, which was usually kept locked?"

"The nurses had keys."

"Which nurses?"

"The ward Sister. But also Sunee's friends had one of their own, privately copied."

"Do you know that for a fact?"

"Only because they told me. I never saw or held the key."

"Was the door open or locked when you went to the store room?"

"It was open."

But the Hunts and Miss Tupper had told him that the door was open after the builder and the architect had left it. Also that the two men had asked for and taken the key from the works department to make their visit to the room, and had returned the key later. Then why had they left the room open? Also Sister Byrnes had gone along to lock the door after Miss Tupper had reported it open.

So the door was unlocked for a comparatively short time that afternoon and at a known time.

"Exactly what time did you go up to the second floor?" Michael asked. "Do you remember and can you prove it?"

Ali, who had been a little comforted by the surgeon's expressed belief in him, answered eagerly.

"Oh, yes, sir. I was finished in my day's work. It was just half after five o'clock."

Five-thirty. But that was impossible. Miss Tupper had looked into the store room just after four. That time was known. Sister Byrnes had looked in, seen nothing wrong, but had not inspected the inner room. That was not later than four-thirty. The room had been locked from then on according to Sister's evidence. So Ali could not have got in at half-past five unless he had had a key himself. Or, grisly thought, unless he had visited the store room earlier than the two Englishmen, unlocked the door with the foreign nurses' key, killed the girl and locked the door again upon leaving. But surely that was impossible? The nurses, her friends, would have spread alarm if Ali had brought them back the key with no Tan Sunee following. Or if neither she nor the key made an appearance they would have reported her missing, before in fact they did so with the discovery of her dead body. And who then unlocked the door? With which key?

No. Ali might be speaking the truth when he swore that the door was unlocked and that he left it so when he had discovered his tormentor dead and fled from the sight in sick horror and deadly fear.

Then was the time wrong, impossible? Had it all happened in that brief hour between four-thirty and five-thirty? Some other so far unknown attacker, avenger, madman? It was all too confusing, too problematical, too far beyond any thought or practice within his own sphere of action, he decided.

"I must be getting along now," he said, speaking kindly but firmly as he was accustomed to do to a recalcitrant patient who refused a necessary operation. "I think I wouldn't add anything about the blackmail to your so-called confession, if I were you, Ali. Only gives the opposition an extra motive for murder, doesn't it? No, don't give up, my dear chap. I believe you, personally. I'm sure Mr. Zimballah will do everything he can. The police in this country really are fair-minded."

He stopped speaking, for the lawyer's hackles had risen at his support of the police. The case was going to be damned difficult, however it went. Well, if his words had tipped Mr. Zimballah on to Ali's side, so much the better. For himself he couldn't care less. The foreign medicals, from his point of view, registrars and housemen and nurses and assistants of various kinds, fell into two main groups, the competent and teachable, however alien their essential outlook, and the incompetent and dangerous, who ought never to have been appointed. Ali Ahmed belonged to the first group. He would continue to support him until he found good reason to do otherwise.

The police held a simpler position. They took it as obvious that the Pakistani pharmacist was the villain in the case and they had only to produce a complete confession with enough material evidence to support it. They encouraged Mr. Zimballah to work on his client over the confession. It was for this that they had allowed Beddoes to join the lawyer in the accused man's cell. There must be no possible excuse for the very active anti-discrimination bodies to mount a campaign on Ahmed's behalf.

All the same Miss Tupper, drat the old bag, had thrown a fairly substantial spanner into the works. Of course it was all nonsense, but it did shake them to find, after Craig's further researches into parish records, that Ray Tilsett was after all a distant cousin of the discharged murderer. Not that he was any closer than that, nor had Miss Tupper identified him; she had seen only the back view. It was his companion, the architect, much younger than Tilsett, whose furiously angry face had so upset the old lady. As her relations the Hunts had said, she had been an actress, she loved drama, she always exaggerated.

"So what did you get from the old national newspapers?" Detective Superintendent Robertson asked Craig.

"Nothing we haven't got on Cat Tilsett himself before from the locals, sir. Both before and after his trial. Except pictures of his wife and child."

"Child!" Robertson was interested. "Go on. What about them?"

"Interview with her after the verdict. Never suspected anything, or would have reported it."

"They often say that."

"Said he always treated her right and loved his little boy, picture of worried looking thin-faced woman and child of about eight."

"Eight," repeated Robertson. "Too young for either of those chaps Miss Tupper saw. Where's this Mrs. Tilsett now, I wonder? Tilsett himself must have given some address at the nick when he left it two years ago."

"Wasn't he ill then, or something?" Craig asked.

"Oh yes, he was. But not yet ill enough. Better look all that up. You didn't find any more about this Mrs. Tilsett, I suppose?"

"I didn't try, sir. You said—"

"O.K. O.K. I'll take it on from there."

Which he did, with a potentially interesting result. He went first to check on all police records again, covering the trial with all the Black Cat's antecedents and family history, his respectable forebears, his promising youth, his wilder development, his later Jekyll and Hyde existence, before his utterly reckless behaviour that ended with his exposure, arrest and conviction. All of which Robertson had studied already and which told him nothing new.

From his next careful re-reading of the local Press he went to the national papers, again in search of early history. Their cover of the trial was rather less interesting than that of the locals, for it dealt with young Mrs. Tilsett only very briefly. Baffled, he was about to give up this line of inquiry, for in his opinion it was sure to prove superfluous, when it occurred to him that one of the nationals, rather given to elaborate research into nasty news dustbins secreting titillating filth, might have been interested in the criminal's release and subsequent history as far as it was known.

He was right. A careful biography had been constructed to prove that criminality is in-born, at least in part, and not wholly due to circumstances, disadvantage and so on. The murderer, Tilsett, had been given every chance of reasonable success in life, but greed and bad temper had led to real sadistic brutality. He had made an early marriage in secret from his parents, soon broken by his outraged wife, who had fled from him with her little son. The paper did not give any names connected with this marriage, nor any detail of the later history of the mother and child. But Detective Superintendent Robertson did an instant sum in his head and came to the conclusion that he had begun to suspect.

"Crawthorne would be about the right age," he said to himself. "Drat that old bag," he repeated in his mind. "I'll have to clear this up, I suppose."

His heart sank. That top-heavy, confused, sluggish, penurious organisation, the National Health Service, perpetually torn by the envy and ambition in many of the auxiliary ranks and by a strong feeling of injustice among the professionals, was never easy to investigate. There were far too many reputations to be defended in the higher ranks of administrators, and conventional suspicions of the police in the lower.

Robertson applied for an interview with the head

Regional Administrator, Sir Frank Pelman. This worthy had recently retired from the upper ranks of the Civil Service, though he'd never been connected in any way with hospitals or indeed the medical profession of any kind, being a healthy old gentleman. He carried a salary about twice that of the average consultant in any branch of the medical profession.

Sir Frank received Detective Superintendent Robertson politely. He had indeed seen the young architect's contract with the Newchester hospitals, including the Isobel Saunders, but it had been signed by the Area Administrator, Mr. Philip Newbury, to whom the detective should apply personally. Was there anything else? – Always ready to help – Hoped there was nothing wrong. The strangled nurse? Yes, dreadful case. But how prompt the police had been. A racialist case, wasn't it? Enmity among different Asian races. No? Well, Mr. Newbury would be able to advise him. Good morning.

Mr. Newbury, warned of the Detective Superintendent's purpose and subject of inquiry by Sir Frank Pelman's office, had briefed himself suitably and was quite ready to cope.

"Young Victor Crawthorne came to us from Liverpool," he said, "where he'd been assistant to a building firm after becoming qualified from Durham."

"Brought up in Durham?" asked Robertson. "Parents lived there?"

"Mother lived there. Also grandparents on her side. I believe the mother died when he was about twelve."

"And the father? Also called Crawthorne?"

Mr. Newbury stared coldly at Robertson, not answering, but as from the start of this conversation becoming more and more wary.

"This is in strict confidence, you understand," the detective said, to encourage the Area Administrator. "No minutes of our meeting. No computer record."

"No," said Mr. Newbury. He felt certain that Robertson had no need to rely on his memory, but had the correct tiny apparatus upon his person to record every word they were saying. He was not going to lay himself open to such an obvious risk.

"I cannot tell you anything more about Victor Crawthorne," he said. "He works very well for us. He gives every satisfaction to our builders. I have never asked him for more details of his upbringing and private life than I have given you and which you can confirm from his record."

With that he sat back, smiling gently and stabbing sharp little holes in his blotter with one of his several pens.

"Thank you," said Robertson and took his leave.

It was the first clear indication in this case of a determined, a necessary, brush-off. He discounted Sir Frank Pelman. A harmless, if useless, old dodderer, even though he did gobble up all that tax-payers' money. But Newbury had given him the strong impetus to follow a clear withdrawal, a negative clue, one that pointed a sign, though it might lead into a cul-de-sac, towards progress.

Craig must go to Liverpool to hunt up Crawthorne's past. Himself to interview the architect re that visit, those several visits, to the second floor of the Isobel Saunders.

But the architect, he found, was out of the country. He was unmarried, he had no family, his time was his own, his leave of absence from his job four weeks in the year.

9

But his interests, as if he needed them to be guarded in his absence, had already received attention, though indirectly. This was noted by the Detective Superintendent, who dealt with the matter.

It came about three days after Robertson's interview with Mr. Newbury and, as was to be expected, through the agency of Miss Tupper. The old lady, (he withdrew his less polite name for her in his mind) was right on the ball and must not be disregarded.

Miss Tupper was intending to ring him up from her own home, a cottage in the country, to which she had been returned by Phyllis Hunt when the surgeon had pronounced her fit to look after herself in the house, but not yet ready to drive her car.

"Do look after yourself, Aunt Amy," Phyl said, having carried in Miss Tupper's bags, opened all the windows, turned on the water and the gas, started up the central heating, checked the fridge and wound the clocks. "I'll give you a ring tonight to make sure you aren't overdoing it. I think we've bought you enough stores for the next three days. I'll be over again on Thursday and take you out to shop for the weekend."

"You're a dear, good girl," said Aunt Amy, kissing her niece affectionately. "Just let me see if the phone's working."

She lifted the receiver and getting a comforting burr, put it down again.

"Of course I'll be all right," she insisted and stood in her doorway, waving and marking time, which had become a firm habit and still recommended by her surgeon.

But when Phyllis's car was out of sight she went in and lay down on her sitting room divan for nearly an hour before she felt capable of unpacking and sorting out the belongings she had brought back from the Hunts' house.

It was while she was upstairs putting away the contents of her suitcase that the telephone bell rang. There was an extension in her bedroom, so she was able to answer it at once.

"Yes?" she said and gave her number.

"Miss Tupper?"

"Yes. Who is speaking?"

Without answering this question the speaker began a long bitter, scurrilous complaint about the invasion of Britain by foreigners, all foreigners who took the bread out of the mouths of our own workers, but more particularly those foreigners who were so foreign as to be scarcely human and were at the same time criminal, going about murdering young girls who had devoted their lives to the sick.

"I think you must be mad," said Aunt Amy in a reasoning voice, "or very sick yourself. But nothing to do with me."

"Very much to do with you, Miss Tupper," the voice said, not at all put off. "This is to warn you not to go on supporting the Paki who murdered Tan Sunee, or else—"

"Oh, go to hell!" cried Miss Tupper, reverting to

the less ladylike speech of her theatrical days.

But a little later, downstairs, making herself a pot of tea, she wondered who it had been who seemed to know so much about the Isobel Saunders murder. True it had been in all the newspapers, local and national, and in the news on radio and television. So all those crazy way-out clubs and associations who resented the so-called New Commonwealth would naturally latch on to any fault they could find against those they longed to exclude from our shores. But why and how did they come to include herself as an enemy?

No, that was far-fetched in the extreme. Then someone at the hospital itself? She remembered what Phyl had told her, having learnt it from Molly Beddoes; that the so-called 'tea lady' had suggested Ali to the police as a possible suspect, not the victim's little friends.

Well, the good woman was prejudiced, but was she likely to go to such lengths as telephoning a threatening message? Or rather, getting a male friend or relation to telephone? Because the voice had been a man's. She was quite sure of that. Cheek! Bloody cheek!

Miss Tupper, sipping her tea, with her feet up on the divan again stretched out her hand to the telephone. The divan was under the window and the telephone was on the window ledge. The window was open. As her left hand grasped the receiver to lift it another hand came up from below the window and covered it, holding it down.

The shock was considerable. Aunt Amy gave a loud and ringing scream (she had always managed convincing screams on stage), and dropped her cup of tea which fell on the carpet beside her without breaking, but emptying its hot contents over her right leg in passing.

A voice, the same, she thought, as the threatening caller's, said from outside, "Go and open the door! Hurry up, or we'll have to break the lock!"

There was nothing for it but to obey, she decided. She found two men standing outside, dressed in shabby, but clean suits, clean shirts and ties, trimmed hair and beards. They moved swiftly the moment the door was open, one to each side of her, taking her arms, pushing her back, then round, one of them kicking the door shut with a foot, before they half pushed, half lifted her back into the little sitting room. They sat her down in a small upright armchair near the fireplace on the opposite side to the divan and secured her to it, at the same time fastening her feet together, also her hands, with a connecting line between hands and feet.

"It's nylon, love," one of the men said, in quite an ordinary voice, neither loud nor unkind. But he proceeded to fasten a broad strip of plaster across her eyes and with that onset of blindness Miss Tupper began to be afraid. But not too much afraid to speak.

"What do you want?" she asked. Her voice trembled, but the words were clear.

"We'd have said if you'd been civil when we rung you just now," the other man answered. She recognised the voice on the phone, the voice below the window.

"Why can't you say now? I don't mind what you take but I can't stay like this for long. I've only just come out of hospital."

"Too bad," said the mild-voiced one. "But we couldn't trust you. Not after you was going to use the blower. Stands to reason."

She cursed herself for not ringing the police at once

from upstairs. But they must have been somewhere near, the call box at the corner of the main road, probably.

She stayed silent, containing her anger, which for most of the time took the place of fear. Not until the trampling about the cottage, up and downstairs, in and out of the four rooms, the small kitchen at the back and the small bathroom above it, came to an end, did fear return.

For the men did not come back into the sitting room, where their search had begun. She heard them come downstairs for the last time, confer in low voices, open the front door, and to her horror, go out shutting it behind them. The Yale lock clicked, she was shut in bound and sightless. Apart from her voice she had no means of summoning help and that, for a long time, she was afraid to use. How could she be sure they were not lurking outside to prevent just that, supposing she was able to free herself sufficiently to get to the telephone. She was thankful she had not uttered a word or a cry while they rummaged her cottage. They might have gagged her if they had really registered the strength and carrying power of her trained scream. There was still a possibility of attracting attention if only she could be sure the men had gone away. Her cottage was not very far away from the main road or from the clutch of houses at the beginning of the village proper. But could she be sure? She dared not risk it.

Trying to think rationally of their outrageous visit she decided that the silence, the suddenness of their appearance must mean that if they had come by car they must have left the vehicle some way off; if by bus they must have got there at least two hours ago and lain in wait after making that telephone call. The distant hum of traffic on the main road was continuous; she was so used to it she hardly registered any separate components. Cars and vans did pass her door from time to time on most days. She would hear them quite clearly but could she be sure they were friend or foe? In the shock and discomfort of finding herself a blind prisoner, she was inclined to think the whole world a potential enemy. She dared not cry out.

She tried to consider what it was the men wanted. It was not difficult to guess. That diatribe about poor young Ali Ahmed, calling him bloody murderer and other terms of racial abuse was clue enough. Somehow they knew she favoured his innocence, so that made her a 'nigger lover' in the old parlance, a 'Paki favourer' now. They could be fanatical right-wing extremists, but they had not spoken as she was aware that misguided groups of aggressors usually did. Except in the initial telephone call. Anyway, it was the 'tea lady' who had denounced Ali Ahmed. Fat, jolly Mrs. Walls. Employing those men? Ganging up with them? Ludicrous! Impossible!

Besides, what evidence was she supposed to be hiding, in favour of the pharmacist? Evidence, the lack of which had held up his committal for trial on the charge of murder. The answer was *none*. So why the attack on her? Because, she realised, somehow, some people must have got to know that she was promoting investigation into the identity and movements of two men, concerned in hospital affairs, who had been near the scene of the crime at about the time it must have been committed. And it was possible that somehow they had discovered she had a very full newspaper coverage in cuttings about a much earlier murder, widely notorious in England and abroad.

With some complacency, in spite of her growing physical discomfort, Miss Tupper knew that the attempt of the opposition, wherever it came from, had been defeated in this instance. They had probably turned her cottage upside down, they must have broken a few locked drawers and cupboards, but they could not have found the bundle of newspaper cuttings because she had providentially told Phyl and Tom to keep them, show them to Mr. Beddoes and possibly to Mr. Nubb, the councillor who seemed to be interested in the murder, and of course to the police. Though if the Force had not already done their own searching of all the records available she would be most surprised. She had developed a certain respect for the way Mr. Robertson was handling the whole business.

As time went on Miss Tupper thought less about the reason and motive behind her present plight and more, increasingly more, of her bodily ills.

She became very thirsty as the hours passed, but not hungry. Appetite vanished as anxiety grew and moreover she had enjoyed a good lunch with Phyllis at Newchester after shopping there for her stores, before driving on to the cottage. But her legs, in their forbidden attitude in the upright chair to which she was fastened, became more and more painful. The several small wounds, freshly healed, began to throb. The surrounding bruises, deep-seated, only partially dispersed, were swelling again as the upward flow of returning blood trying to make its way through new courses without the help of muscle activity or gravity, was checked, held back and forced to spread into the surrounding tissues. She knew her ankles were swelling rapidly, that the nylon ligature, so strong, so utterly unwielding, was soon biting unmercifully. She could only pray for help to come before the results of her operation were ruined utterly and she was reduced to a permanent cripple.

During the evening the telephone rang twice. Miss Tupper swore the first time. It must be Phyllis; she could not answer it but her niece would conclude she had gone out to see her friends in the village. The second time, she wept, but comforted herself in the end that it was Phyl again, who might wonder why she still did not answer, perhaps wonder enough to come out again or send Tom. But nothing happened, no rescue came.

In desperation she wondered if it was possible to tip her chair over on its side on to the floor. The carpet was fairly thick; though still bound together she ought to be able to stretch her knees so that her legs would be straight and horizontal. But she could not see her surroundings. She could not discover how far she would have to fall, what might happen to her head and shoulder. She could not lift her arms to help herself, since they were tied by that miserable nylon, not only together but by an extension to her ankle ligature.

She tried once or twice to rock the chair, pressing her feet to the ground, but only gave herself a fright when it tipped jerkily before rocking back, scraping one ankle as it did so. She decided to give up the obvious dangers of such efforts, to endure as best she could until the morning, if need be, when the milkman was sure to call, perhaps the postman too. Unless the vicar or his wife came in quite soon, having heard she was back. But that was not likely, for she had not taken the trouble to tell them when it would be.

Later on, before she began to doze from sheer exhaustion, she found herself reciting aloud from parts in the plays she had most enjoyed playing. Usually in provincial tours, or provincial repertory. Among the parts that came back to her were some of the more poignant lines from 'The Duchess of Malfi', in which she had understudied the duchess and though her principal had never missed a performance the run had been a long one in an outlying London theatre before the war. She had enjoyed her weekly rehearsal as the duchess; she had been young and still hopeful. Now, bound and sightless and alone, the Duchess of Malfi's Jacobean agony seemed most appropriate. It relieved her of much of the stress of her own predicament; she slept from time to time; the pain in her legs grew less as the pressure mounted and they became dangerously numb.

When Phyllis Hunt rang up her aunt as promised and got no answer, she did indeed decide that Aunt Amy had gone out to make her number with the vicar, perhaps, whose wife had been attentive with flowers at the Isobel Saunders.

But she did not bother to ring again. Miss Tupper had too often stressed her ability to look after herself at the cottage. And the peace and quiet at home had been really very welcome, as Tom was the first to remark when he got back from the office that evening.

The second call had been from the police. Detective Superintendent Robertson had already decided that he must match Miss Tupper's press cuttings with his own findings and having learned that she had gone home, wanted to fix a meeting with her at the cottage, where she could produce them for him. He came to the same conclusion over her not answering the call, putting off a repeat until the next morning.

But both the police and Phyllis had their answer by seven-thirty. It was the milkman in his electric van, rattling Miss Tupper's gate as he unfastened it with a couple of milk bottles in one hand, who roused her to sufficient energy to call out her need for rescue.

The Hunts' car was overtaken by the police car exceeding the speed limit with siren blaring as it swept up the village street. The milkman was still at the cottage, administering first aid to Miss Tupper in the shape of brandy and water from her cupboard while he boiled a kettle to make tea. He had untied her hands and feet, but she was still seated in the chair and refused to leave it for sanitary reasons, she said, which, being a family man, he understood and respected. He had peeled the plaster back from the sides and below her eyes, but felt too unnerved by the swollen lids and reddened eye-balls to wrench it off her eyebrows. He had turned it over and stuck it on her forehead until a more expert hand could deal with it.

Robertson did not waste time explaining matters to the milkman nor did he attempt to interview Miss Tupper about the press cuttings, beyond learning where they now were. He simply ordered an ambulance.

The milkman was thanked very warmly and went away to continue his round, considerably delayed, but well worth it, the housewives felt, for they had not had such an exciting, first hand account of criminal goings-on for years. Without the dead hand of the tele and the papers grinding it up into the same words every time, they agreed.

So, by mid-morning, Miss Tupper found herself back in the Isobel Saunders, on the second floor again, but in a different room, with the same surgeon, furious at the outrage committed on his patient, considerably worried by the probable injury to her legs. There were the same little nurses, the same 'tea lady'.

But not Sister Byrnes. A new Sister, more amply built and about forty, much less strained-looking than Byrnes, came to commiserate and fuss over her soon after her arrival, while a little cream-faced, green-clad nurse watched from wary black eyes.

Sister Byrnes, Miss Tupper was told, had left the ward, as a result of her own special request, the new Sister explained, but moved by management, Mrs. Walls confided, because she could no longer control the foreign nurses. Sister Byrnes was now working in the Casualty Department of Out Patients.

10

When the police had gathered a full account of the assault on Miss Tupper, backed by their inspection of the havoc wrought in her cottage, they came to the obvious conclusion that this had been no casual burglary, but a carefully thought out search for something somebody wanted. Wanted badly enough to risk a heavy penalty for injury both to person and property.

The attempt had failed, the victim and the police agreed, for various reasons, the most important being that what they sought was not at the cottage, namely that bundle of press cuttings that Aunt Amy had given to her niece, asking her to pass them on to Detective Superintendent Robertson. If either of the two men involved had been less intent upon frightening the old lady into giving them what they were sent to get, and less vindictive when she refused to be frightened, she would probably have told them that a search was useless, the papers were not there. But they would not have believed her, of course. Hired thugs had muscles, not brains.

Miss Tupper hoped they would not be paid money for their mission, though a failure; Robertson told her he hoped they would get payment of a different kind, if he could lay his hands on them. Various sources that he did not specify had already suggested one or two rough characters known to be available for nasty little jobs of intimidation, profitable as a rule. They had just picked a loser in Miss Tupper. It was in their nature to complain of this as an injury to themselves, not to her. Also to be full of their complaint to their cronies, who might lead a double life as police informers. All very well, but who could possibly be the employer? The obvious name was Tilsett, usually a most efficient person. Unless—

Detective Sergeant Craig brought a partial success back from Durham. The young architect's family, or rather his mother and grandparents, had in fact lived there, all named Crawthorne. The architect had told the whole truth about his upbringing in the northern city.

But how was it possible for his mother, Mrs. Crawthorne, to keep her father's name after her marriage? Had she married a cousin of the same name, or had she reverted to her maiden name after the break-up of that marriage? The architect might know and could be asked when he returned from Spain. His mother certainly had died when he was twelve and his education had been continued by the grandparents. But these were now also dead.

Craig had, however, found some surviving friends of the family who knew of a Mr. Tilsett, an occasional visitor, who had come north to see the boy during his adolescence. They had not considered him a relation, more in the nature of a guardian or perhaps a godfather or family benefactor. For it was generally considered that the Crawthornes were rather badly off. There was universal admiration for the way the boy had succeeded by hard work as well as by natural talent. Again, all these points could be confirmed and explained by Crawthorne himself.

Robertson took Craig with him to visit Miss Tupper. They found her on the second floor of the Isobel Saunders occupying the same part of the ward as before, but a different room. She had been in poor shape upon arrival, the police were told, but was now, two days later, well enough to see visitors other than her niece.

"Quite at home, Miss Tupper," the Detective Superintendent said cheerfully, but added in a more serious tone, "and looking a great deal better than when I last saw you, thank goodness."

"Thank you, I'm quite recovered in myself," she answered him. "But my poor old legs are not, by any means. Those damned ruffians tied me up in a sitting position. I couldn't explain I had to have my legs straight, horizontal, if not in action. They wouldn't have understood or paid a blind bit of notice. Primitive savages, the pair of them!"

"It's not a serious setback, I hope," said Robertson. "I mean," (seeing opposition growing in Miss Tupper's face) "not a permanent thing – the operation result – not ruined?"

"Perhaps not," Miss Tupper grudged, for she resented her surgeon's expression of relief for the welfare of his handiwork, taking little account of her feelings. "But it means going back several stages in the treatment, all that rigmarole of marking time and resting between bouts of exercises. Too tiresome. Such a waste of effort earlier. I ought to be driving the car again by now. This new Sister is very sympathetic, a great comfort."

As a matter of fact, Miss Tupper had spent the first twenty-four hours after her rescue under deep sedation for delayed shock. This had not put off the physiotherapist, who had started massage of the unfortunate legs, though voluntary movement was not possible.

On the other hand the new Sister was a welcome contrast to Mary Byrnes, with her ill-concealed feud with the nurses, and her very open distress and shame after the tragedy to one of them. Sister Flore, a few years older than Byrnes, with a comfortable maternal figure and round face, had permed fair hair holding up her Sister's cap at a jaunty angle that the dark Irish woman's black straight locks never achieved. In her blue Sister's uniform she seemed hardly aware that anything was, or had been, amiss with her ward.

Miss Tupper took the fresh encouragements gratefully and with pleasure. She decided from the start that she would not discuss the murder with Sister Flore and would resist any mention of it if possible. The whole thing had become too complicated and as Phyl and Tom kept insisting, it was really not her business. And yet the police did seem to take her into consideration in the matter, or why had they come to see her again, so soon after that attack on her?

"They must have wanted those press cuttings," she said. "Didn't my niece hand them over to you?"

"Yes, of course."

Robertson described the whole outcome of his inquiries into the press coverage of the recent murder, the problems of the Tilsett family connections and the possible link with Victor Crawthorne. They were waiting for the young man to come back from Spain.

"But why wait?" Miss Tupper asked. "If you think

the architect Crawthorne might possibly be the Cat's *son,* which is what you're hinting at, isn't it?"

"I hope I have made no such positive hint," Robertson said severely.

"Rubbish!" Aunt Amy said, laughing. "Of course you did. Well, surely you people are still in touch with the old murderer, know his address, keep some sort of tabs on him, even if he is now a pampered pensioner—"

"No," said Robertson, interrupting this flow of speculation. "No, Miss Tupper. The Black Cat died three months ago, of cancer. He was allowed to leave prison two years ago because he was suffering from the disease and not expected to serve any more of his sentence, which had an initial limit of fifteen. He went from the prison hospital to another provincial one and has been in and out ever since. He had three operations altogether and all the modern drugs and treatments. Result, the usual average one, I've been told. He was allowed to use a false name, at his very insistent request. This was allowed on humanitarian grounds, to keep the Press off him and was used at the hospital where he died, but not on the death certificate, which went to his next-of-kin."

"Very right and proper," said Miss Tupper. She had been sobered by the Detective Superintendent's story and now, strangely enough, felt a sudden disgust with herself for her sudden burst of intuition, memory, dramatic impulse, or whatever it had been, that had dragged the dead man into an inquiry that by no means could contain him, but might injure others quite innocent, but unhappily connected in a family way.

She saw that the two detectives were watching her

closely. She said, "I've been a fool and you must have been thinking that all along. I'm sorry."

"No." Robertson spoke quietly. "Tilsett was a thoroughly bad character, born that way. He had a happy home, he was a bright kid, but bad. I believe some are. He paid for it all right. Ten years inside and two in hospital having a pretty good hell. What really matters is if you saw that badness, as it might be, passed on to the next generation. I mean if you saw—"

"If I saw the evil inherited, or perhaps just its like in another unrelated person?"

"That sort of thing." Robertson was not quite sure what he did mean.

Craig thought they were both hedging in a pointless effort to avoid an obvious fact. The old girl had a good memory. She liked to read the papers for stories of crime and violence as everyone else did. She recognised a face wearing the expression of a chap blowing his top in a big way. She'd mixed it up with two photographs, one of a notorious criminal, the other—

"Miss Tupper," he said, seeing his chief and the old lady had bogged themselves down in the higher ideology, as you might call it. "I think you said before that you'd made a mistake about the photos. When you met Mr. Tilsett and Mr. Crawthorne you were sure you'd never seen Tilsett before, but the younger one, you thought you had. Not looking angry, just normal."

"Yes, I did." She was relieved to change the subject of original sin, in which she most reluctantly believed. "Yes, I'm sure I've seen a picture of him quite recently. Certainly not at home, I mean not anywhere in a friend's house or in the village. Not at the Hunts'. Possibly, I suppose, here in the hospital."

"Where he works," said Robertson slowly, exchanging a quick look with Craig. "Though you wouldn't expect to see a photo of him in his office at the works department. Unless he'd made a friend of one of the typists."

"I certainly never visited the works department," said Miss Tupper, laughing. "Why on earth should I? I was never anywhere except in this ward, both parts of it, of course, when my walking was extended."

"So it must have been in a patient's room," said Craig.

"Or somewhere belonging to the staff," added Robertson, remembering the stories, never proved true or false, of Crawthorne's traffic with the oriental nurses.

"There isn't any proper staff room," Miss Tupper said. "They sit about in groups in all sorts of unlikely places, washrooms, kitchens, stores—"

She remembered the fatal store room and the part of it in constant, most undesirable use. She reddened and was silent.

"Let us know if it comes back to you," Robertson said, signalling to Craig to go no further. Aunt Amy was pleased to be left alone again.

Soon after they had gone, Mrs. Walls, the tea lady, appeared with the usual tray, the over-full coarse pottery cup, strong Indian tea slopping into the saucer, the dry scone, split and buttered on one side only, the meagre slice of packaged swiss roll.

As it was only half-past three and she had not been able to have her usual after-lunch doze, she was not feeling strong enough or hungry enough to welcome this unattractive meal.

But Mrs. Walls was her usual motherly self, beaming

encouragement. So Aunt Amy said, smiling in her turn, "I've just had the Law in again, Mrs. Walls. I feel whacked. Do you think, just this once, I might have a whole pot, not just one cup?"

Mrs. Walls gave a great, throaty guffaw.

"You don't know what you're asking, dear. The pots are giant size for the open wards. You wouldn't get one to fit on a tray, much less light enough to carry all this way. Single rooms, like this, has an urn."

"Well, perhaps a second cup," suggested Aunt Amy, disappointed.

Mrs. Walls, mildly affronted by this hint of weight-throwing, on the part of a non-urgent case at that, began to stiffen. Patients getting their board and lodging free ought to have some consideration for voluntary workers, didn't they?

"I'll see what I can do," she said coldly and added, "Now we've got Sister Flore the ward doesn't hardly know itself and a very good job too."

"You mean discipline?" Aunt Amy asked, finding the explanation obscure and surely unrelated to second cups of tea for thirsty patients.

"That's right." Mrs. Walls' face had changed. The smile of goodwill had been exchanged for a rather disagreeable grin of triumph. "Them Chinks don't know what's biting them. Impudent little bitches, the lot of them."

Miss Tupper had been aware that the foreign nurses took a racialist view of Mrs. Walls. She had seen them making their own kind of fun of her, imitating her ponderous walk, her lamentably roguish eye movements. It was natural that the feeling was reciprocated. But as strongly as this change in Mrs. Walls suggested?

"You mean that Sister Flore is severe with them?"

"Better than Mary Byrnes, but not enough yet. She'll get their number though, which Miss Byrnes never did. Too scared of them, I wouldn't wonder."

"Really? Why scared?"

Mrs. Walls did not answer this directly.

"You can't altogether blame her. She knew of their goings on, but she daren't report it. So she felt responsible when one of them got what she deserved. Silly, that. What else could you expect from a Paki, isn't he?"

"Do you mean the pharmacist, Mr. Ahmed? It hasn't been proved yet that he did it."

She was thinking of the possible police findings. Mrs. Walls was scornful, emphatically so.

"You mean no one's guilty till the jury brings in a positive verdict? All my eye and Betty Martin. This man's as guilty as hell. Stands to reason, doesn't it? Sort of thing a native would do, though why he didn't use one of his drugs out of the pharmacy I don't understand. Leaving the poor kid lying there for her friends to find. Horrible!"

Miss Tupper listened to all this in disgust, particularly the false ending. Mrs. Walls was *not* sorry that Tan Sunee had been killed; she was glad. Her only anxiety was that Ali Ahmed might be found not guilty. At any rate this nasty conversation must end. Racialism either way round, and it seemed to be rampant in both directions in the Isobel Saunders, was dreadful. Discussions such as the one Mrs. Walls had started could not, must not, be allowed. She did not attempt to answer the tea lady's outburst. She just looked at her, smiled what she knew must be an artificial grimace and said "What about that extra cuppa, Mrs. Walls? I'm truly very thirsty."

Mrs. Walls quite literally shook herself, let her stiffened features relax, said "I'll see what I can do" and walked away as fast as her heavy weight and her flat feet would let her.

In about twenty minutes she was back, with a brimming cup, no explanations, no further gossip.

Miss Tupper did not try to renew conversation. She had been very surprised to find such complexities in a character she had hitherto taken for granted. Voluntary helpers, slightly comic figures both physically and morally – the do-gooder class, nicer-side-of. Entirely disinterested, in the real sense of that often misused word, she told herself smugly. But what a travesty of the real Mrs. Walls! There had been genuine passion in her expressions of racial hatred. She had been pleased the girl had died; as pleased as in a less civilised world she might have killed her with her own hands as a feared and hated stranger.

Shocked by this thought Aunt Amy's usual sense of drama produced the freshly exciting thought that possibly, just possibly, Mrs. Walls had given herself away. Gruesome idea! Grisly pleasure! Miss Tupper rebuked herself severely. She forbade any further speculation in this direction. She would mention it to no one. She would *not* ring up Mr. Robertson nor Phyl. Later on, enjoying an unusually appetising light supper, she decided to write down some figures relating to times and attendances of hospital auxiliaries with their appearance on the second floor wards.

Sister Flore had established a regular habit of visiting each patient on the second floor before she went off duty for the day. She found Miss Tupper flushed, a little over-excited and over-anxious. She remembered the police visit and regretted it. She liked Miss Tupper: she ticked her case sheet to authorise a repeat of her late night tranquilliser. She remembered what the voluntary worker Mrs. Walls had said at the end of the tea round.

"That old lady that had her house burgled and came in again for her legs, she's a bit unhinged in my opinion. What with the murder of that foreign nurse. She didn't ought to be back in the same ward in my opinion. Better off in her own home, I reckon."

"With the house still in a mess? Surely not, Mrs. Walls?"

"Well, with that niece of hers, why not? She went to them before. Doing herself no good with all those questions she's forever asking."

Mrs. Walls had gone before Sister Flore had been able to ask her what questions precisely Miss Tupper had asked. But of course they must have something to do with the police interview. Sister Flore was not inclined to take Mrs. Walls seriously.

On the other hand as time passed Miss Tupper took the tea lady very seriously indeed. For, with her walks renewed and longer ones at that, which meant crossing the landing and penetrating the other half of the ward, she came more and more into contact with the little nurses in their smart green uniforms, their caps snowy on their shining black hair, their cream-coloured faces unsmiling as she passed them. Unsmiling too, as Mrs. Walls passed them, shrinking away, turning their backs, no longer laughing together, tending rather to slip instantly behind doors as it might be trees in a dense jungle.

11

Mr. Nubb, correct, conscientious, hardworking Mr. Nubb, was becoming increasingly anxious. His disturbing idea, triggered off by that unexpected, unwanted offer of help in the maintenance of his house, was becoming an obsession. It lay at the back of his mind always. But instead of lying quietly there, firmly rejected and so fading away quite gently and painlessly, it kept rushing to the surface, a bloated outrageous thing, exploding for acknowledgment in all its disgraceful features, for explanation, which could only lead to disaster in one direction, to acute personal embarrassment in the other.

Never had Mr. Nubb felt so utterly alone over a difficult problem. Usually a quiet reference to one of his superiors on the Council when he felt perplexed would bring relief in the form of guidance. By superiors he meant those more forceful members who did all the talking at committee meetings of the whole Council and acted as chairmen of the several sub-committees on two of which Mr. Nubb sat. His membership of the Finance and General Purposes Committee only added to his troubles, because the chairman of the F. and G.P. was the one who had made that very guarded suggestion that the builder Tilsett's prices were very competitive, very reasonable indeed.

How very reasonable they were had been brought home to him by his wife, Dorothy, who was a friend on constant visiting terms with the councillor's wife.

"Do you know what Jessie's just told me?" she said, starting the subject, as was her habit, with a question she knew Gerald could not answer.

"No. What?" he asked, not paying much attention. Jessie's pronouncements were always a mystery, both before and also after explanation.

But not this time.

"Well, you know they had their greenhouse wrecked by that dreadful wind in the spring. Tornado, the papers called it."

"Which it wasn't," said Mr. Nubb, roused by this piece of nonsense. "A tornado is a type of hurricane they have in—"

"Well, never mind that." Dorothy was anxious to come to the really astonishing part of her story. "Jessie says replacing the greenhouse – all the glass broken and the frame bent in all directions – was going to be beyond them. They began to go into prices and that, and it would cost the earth they found. But when they asked advice from that Mr. Tilsett – you know – Newchester Builders – he came up with a wonderful idea. He had a greenhouse a client had ordered and then for some reason or other was obliged to leave the district. He'd let it go to them at half price and wouldn't charge them for bringing it round to their place if they'd instal it themselves. Well, of course there wouldn't be any trouble over that. Jessie's nephew works for Newchester Builders. He usually gives them a hand in the garden when they need it. They're both getting on a bit."

"Yes," said Mr. Nubb. "They are, aren't they?

When did you say this happened? In the spring, was it?"

"Oh I don't remember if Jessie said exactly when. Why d'you want to know?"

He could not explain that, because it was just after Easter that the question of the extension and alterations for the new operating theatres at the hospital had been put up to the F. & G.P. committee. Newchester was expected to pass the plans since the site belonged to the town, and to contribute to the expense as part of the charity that originally donated the hospital. In fact the committee had passed the plans and the job had then been voted to go to Tilsett's firm. He himself had been one of those voting in favour, principally because it meant that Newchester men would be employed in the work.

Hearing this news of such deadly import Mr. Nubb felt defeated for the moment, but now cowed. He could hardly bring up to the chairman of the F. & G.P. the question of perks, inducements rather, to councillors by a reputable local building firm when the chairman had received a signal favour from that firm. Had the offer of the secondhand greenhouse been made before or after the meeting that confirmed or rather recommended giving Tilsett the contract? Well, did that matter? The actual contract had to be signed by the Council itself. Rubber stamped? Of course. But still a recommendation could be defeated; a contract, unsigned, did not commit the Council to payment. Whereas the greenhouse had probably been paid for. Or not paid for. What about insurance? Had the former greenhouse been insured? Mr. Nubb's head whirled.

He felt unjustly frustrated. He did not know any of

his fellow councillors well enough to ask them confidential questions. Particularly on money matters.

But he did feel entitled to see the actual accounts relating to projects originally handled by his committee. He had already seen most of them attached as separate sheets to his personal copies of the minutes of their meetings. With persistence and an amiable patience that appealed to the young women of the department he visited, he managed to extract copies of these published accounts and also the scrutiny of the actual sums paid, signed and paid over to the various bodies that had done the actual work of issuing demands for, and receiving rates in respect of, roads and car parks, the caring of, renovating, demolishing, council housing and all the rest of the public work the impoverished citizen used to be responsible for personally, but now had to pay exorbitantly for others to do instead.

Mr. Nubb was astonished at the volume of material for his study. He was also hardly astonished, but very gravely disturbed to find his growing suspicions partly confirmed. A great deal of business had gone to the firm of Newchester Builders Ltd.; a very large sum in payments at fairly frequent intervals had been made to that firm.

But on the face of it not a single project could have been illegally undertaken or overpaid for. Only, when Mr. Nubb had made out a list of all the transactions and taken it home with him to study in peace, after returning the records, the folders, the files, the computer details, to their guardians, did his unease grow, together with a feeling that he could not give up at this point, but must go further.

After all, those young women in the records and

accounts departments had not been totally unobservant. One or two had been inquisitive, he remembered.

"You are working very hard, Mr. Nubb," decided the tall one with hair too long for its dull mouse colour and its greasy tendency to fall in clotted strings over her eyes. "What's it all in aid of?"

"Wouldn't you like to know?" Mr. Nubb returned, trying to achieve a roguishness so uncharacteristic it almost frightened his questioner. She faded away quickly while her colleagues laughed and one of them said, "Mr. Nubb's a councillor, aren't you, Mr. Nubb? He's checking the way the money goes so they can put up the rates. Aren't you, Mr. Nubb?"

Another said, "He wants to record the figures for a foreign power. He's making a microfilm with one of those transistor cameras in a coat button." She had a liking for spy stories and enjoyed showing off her understanding or otherwise of the expertise.

To all this he had just smiled and told them nothing at all. Though it did occur to him that he was engaged upon a form of spying reprehensible, perhaps, since it concerned his fellow councillors. But very necessary if he had to confirm with real figures his growing suspicions of corruption.

One conclusion was obvious. The Newchester Builders had been more favoured with Council contracts than any other firm local or country-wide. Also everything they had handled was in some way connected with the National Health Service. Not only with the Isobel Saunders, but with the Newchester General, with the even larger establishment in the county town, with the various special clinics in the area.

Therefore, argued the methodical, conscientious Mr. Nubb, the next person to consult in the matter, must surely be that rather shadowy figure who administered the N.H.S. in and around Newchester, Area Administrator, didn't they call him? And who might that be, he wondered.

In the old days it had been plain enough. There had been Dr. Masters, M.B., B.S., D.P.H. A qualified doctor with a diploma in public health. He had been the Medical Officer of Health. He had been perfectly capable of dealing with local clinics for chest diseases, maternity in all its aspects, child welfare, the health and well-being of schoolchildren, immunisation against certain diseases, early diagnosis of TB, with public display of tests in travelling vans fully equipped for the purpose. Also the notification and control of certain epidemic diseases, notification of venereal disease and clinics for treatment. All this with a few Health visitors and the help of the District Nurses and Midwives.

It would have been easy to talk to Dr. Masters whom he had known personally and admired as a highly qualified professional man. Dr. Masters knew all about the medical side of his job from the public health point of view. He did not deal with individual patients and their personal ills, but with a section of the human race in a community, its needs and protection from enemy viruses and bacteria, from ignorance, poverty, poor mental and physical constitutions. He was not overburdened with, or hounded by, committees of management. He would have understood, with sympathy, Councillor Nubb's anxiety about the possible exploitation of the rate payer and the tax payer by a tradesman seducing certain of his fellow councillors for monetary gain.

That would have been easy with the independent professional mind and outlook of Dr. Masters. But who should he appeal to now among that multitude of overlapping officials, known as administrators? A long, important-sounding name for an amorphous group of individuals, often untrained in any specific craft, mental or manual, unlearned in any academic discipline, unless it might be that fanciful unscientific mixture of ideals and faulty statistics called sociology, mixed with the more imaginative, perverse, equally faulty speculations of so-called social psychology.

Mr. Nubb knew that his careful researches led him towards this tangled, perhaps impenetrable thicket. He suspected that any direct contact with it would not be welcome. Surely to God there was more than enough overlapping already. His prime duty was to his own Council, to Newchester. He could only expect defeat and probably a curt command by the N.H.S. hierarchy to mind his own business.

After a few days of abject withdrawal, during which time Nubb brooded more and more upon his own cowardice, another neighbourly report from his wife brought the matter to a head, destroying every wish to bury his fears and doubts.

Dorothy was bubbling with excitement.

"You'll never guess—" she began, but seeing the gloom deepen on Gerald's face she hurried on. "No, I know that's a silly thing to say. Don't try to."

To her surprise, he interrupted her to say, "Of course, I can't guess until I know what the problem is. Go on, Dot."

"It's not a problem. At least, I suppose you could call it that, in a way."

"Get on, dear. Get *on*!"

"You know how awful the Biggs' drive has got since those ghastly frosts last winter and spring. Pot holes all over. Ruination for any car tyres, I've thought. Well, they've got workmen in putting down a new surface. All over, not just filling up the holes like Mr. Biggs did all summer with ash and cinders and that."

"Well?" asked Mr. Nubb, as she paused for breath, though he had guessed what was coming and anger began to stir under the heavy reluctance he had been piling on it.

"Well, how can they possibly afford to put on that tar stuff? But then Glad told me who were doing the job. Now, can you guess?"

"Yes, I can," Mr. Nubb cried out, so sharply that Dorothy, who was as usual tipping her chair as she spoke, very nearly overturned it. "Tilsett, of course! Another special price, I've no doubt."

"Yes," said Dorothy, who was no fool in business matters. She had acted as secretary for several years in her father's business before she married the comfortably secure Gerald Nubb with his fixed permanent job, with pension building up, and a town councillor, already re-elected twice.

"Yes," she repeated. "Must be doing well, those Newchester Builders, mustn't they?"

"Yes," said Mr. Nubb, "following the greenhouse you told me of. But I think you'd better not stress the story, if you get me, Dot."

"O.K. I won't," she said, understanding and pleasantly surprised that she did so. Among her friends it was already a joke, that and one or two other tales like it. But Gerald was taking it more seriously, so she decided to go along with him, and not repeat any more jokes of this rather dubious kind.

As for Mr. Nubb, this new benefaction, even though not confirmed, did away with all his hesitation. The racket, if such it really was, must be checked; hopefully exposed, though this would be very difficult. It might be impossible to bring Tilsett and his partners or promoters, whoever they were, to book without tearing apart the Council and perhaps the town with it.

Mr. Nubb got a list of the N.H.S. administrators, their levels and areas of action, their names and addresses. He rightly guessed, as Beddoes the surgeon had not, that Sir Frank Pelman would refuse to have anything to do with the matter. With his successful past behind him he would not fail in any standard exercise of passing the buck. So the most hopeful individual down the line would naturally be Mr. Newbury who lived and worked in Newchester itself. Mr. Nubb rang up his office and made an appointment to see the official at his convenience. He gave his own office address and said the object of the required interview was a matter concerned with the N.H.S. He refused to describe it further to the sharp-voiced female at the other end of the line, but he got his appointment fixed.

Mr. Newbury was a good listener in that he did not interrupt the councillor's long and in the end faltering exposition of his suspicions and fears. He had risen to his feet to greet Mr. Nubb with a limp handshake. The appointment was for a mid-morning session so it was automatic that coffee followed at once, though sipping very hot fluid did not help Mr. Nubb, though it gave Mr. Newbury an occupation that seemed to absorb him completely.

However, the councillor managed to stumble through a fairly coherent account of the various benefactions enjoyed by certain of his colleagues and conferred in each and every case by Newchester Builders. It would appear that each time these well – gifts really, weren't they, had been made, meetings of the Council committee upon which he sat himself had passed recommendations giving important contracts for works to be undertaken by the firm. All those works, Mr. Nubb said in conclusion, had been for works in the health sphere, hospital, clinics and the like.

"Ordered by Newchester Council, I understand," said Mr. Newbury.

"In so far as planning permission, local charities run by the town or by a citizen in the past, or where the rates are concerned you could call it that, I suppose," answered Mr. Newbury, a bit nettled by this apparent slowness of uptake. "But these works belong overall to the N.H.S. which is not a corporation on its own but part of a government ministry."

"Your Council's actions lie quite outside my area of competence," went on Mr. Newbury blandly. "Or, have you anything further to add?"

"I have a great deal to add," Mr. Nubb answered, now thoroughly roused. Passing the buck in the end he had already anticipated. Passing it before the coffee was even cool enough to drink, apart from sipping, was the end. The very end. Or else quite a different beginning.

"Look here," he said, in a new kind of voice which startled the administrator into swallowing a mouthful of coffee the wrong way, with subsequent breathless choking, retching, watering eyes, running nose, speechlessness.

Mr. Nubb went on speaking, but more quietly.

There was a table between him and his adversary, as he now considered Newbury, so he could not easily slap the other on the back to relieve him. Nor did it ever do much good to help. He went on explaining however that bribing councillors with material advantage of any kind was a criminal offence, for the one who proposed it and also for the recipient. It was a very serious matter.

"I entirely agree," gasped Mr. Newbury.

"I thought, as the very lucrative contracts we have voted for the Newchester Builders, whose prices are if anything above those of their contenders, have been all of a medical nature, I mean a Health Service nature, you ought to be made aware of it. Should it come to an official investigation, which God forbid."

"Amen," said Mr. Newbury fervently.

"You have no reason to find fault with these builders' work?"

"None whatever."

"You know the managing director?"

"Mr. Tilsett? I have met him, yes."

"You would know, would you, if he appeared to be unusually well off?"

Mr. Newbury was affronted.

"I know better than to be offensively inquisitive," he said rather grandly.

Mr. Nubb saw that he would get nowhere with this character. He wore the armour of his appointed position. He was prepared to use the weapons that went with it, the deadly machines of delay, muddle, misunderstanding, apathy.

It was useless, but he made a last appeal, even as he was getting up from his chair.

"Well," he said, speaking as if he represented the

view of his whole committee, "we are becoming anxious. If Tilsett is engaged in attempted corruption on behalf of himself or of a gang who put up the bribes and give him a percentage when he lands a contract, we are determined to winkle it out. And I do hope you find yourself behind us in that, Mr. Newbury. Now that you know what we suspect."

"Of course. Of course." Mr. Newbury was on his feet too, still a little breathless, the redness caused by his paroxysm fading from his face, leaving it paler than usual.

"And our conversation is confidential, of course?"

"Perfectly."

They parted with another limp handshake. Mr. Nubb had a feeling the interview had been less profitable than he had hoped. But not unexpected. No use sighing for the old order, but what good was this modern set up? Surely it was several steps in the wrong direction? Dr. Masters, now—

Better not think about old Masters. But wouldn't he turn in his grave if he'd listened to Newbury getting ready to shovel a problem under the carpet. Newbury, who enjoyed a salary more than twice the size of his own surgeon neighbour, Beddoes, and that he knew for a fact.

12

Victor Crawthorne travelled back to England three days after Mr. Nubb's interview with the N.H.S. administrator. The plane, mid-week, overnight, cheap return, landed at Heathrow in a light mist before dawn. Vic shivered as he walked up the closed but unheated corridor from the runway. He stopped once or twice to look back through the glass at the distant rounded belly of the monster in which he had dozed the middle of the night away, high above Europe.

The last two weeks had been marvellous, fantastic. Not his first visit to Spain, but the first, anywhere, in such comfort, such luxury of food and surroundings, such company.

Of course he had been very, very careful. He never had found it easy to make new friends and just now he had decided, backed by Uncle Ray, that he had better not make any real friends at all. Particularly girls. Not friends, that is. The occasional contact – naturally. But there again, with the right money in the wallet, the girls matched the rest of his enjoyments, his contacts, his service.

So Crawthorne made his leisurely way into the airport building, showed his passport, retrieved his bag, joined the queue for 'nothing to declare' and presently found himself released from all authority, thrown back, a free nonentity, into the endlessly moving swarm of the unsorted.

He was of middle height, but tall enough, because he held himself upright and straight, to have a clear sight of labelled doors and the directions attached to them. He began to walk slowly towards the nearest source of food.

There had been coffee on the plane during the last hour of the flight and cereal or biscuits. He felt he would like to have a real breakfast before leaving the airport. Before he had to count the cost again of everything he did or ate. When he landed he had decided to spend the rest of that day in London, do a theatre, eat at a famous restaurant. But when he had changed his remaining pesetas back into English money he knew this would not be possible. The god-given bonus had done him proud, but not enough to live in his home country as well as he had in that sparkling, delicious dreamland he had just so reluctantly left.

The second slap of reality was dealt him at the doors of the first restaurant he found. No cooked breakfast, he read, on a hand-written notice. Staff shortage, due to industrial trouble.

Disgusted, he turned away. At the bookstall the first editions of the morning papers had arrived and told him more. A police raid to arrest a clutch of thieves in the catering department had so incensed the rest of the staff that they had walked out at once.

"Silly buggers!" Vic muttered under his breath.

"Which lot?" asked Ray Tilsett behind him.

Crawthorne swung round. What the devil—?

"Yes, it's me," Tilsett said. "Didn't they give you breakfast on the way?"

"Nothing really."

"And this lot's walked out. The lot, including the cafeterias, though they say those'll be working in an hour or so."

Victor groaned. He was not particularly pleased to see the builder. For two whole weeks he had been free of that doubtful help, doubtful influence. For two weeks he had lived the life of a prosperous, upstanding, successful professional man, welcomed by other professional or business men. He had been openly admired for his youth, because it suggested either an unusually good brain and ability or else an unusually generous backer. He had told them he worked for a corporation. That went down well on the whole, because the only two other Englishmen were doctors and the rest, including the Americans, had very hazy ideas about what a British corporation really was.

However, it was pointless to brood over the comfort of good, expensive living in the new rugged, uncaring, radical atmosphere of his homeland. Instead he turned away from the closed restaurant with an irritated shrug of his broad shoulders.

"I'm hungry," he said.

"All right. Pipe down, I'm thinking."

"What are you doing here, anyway?"

Victor was puzzled. He could remember no plans for their future that required a conference at Heathrow, immediately after his arrival there. Unless—

"Nothing wrong, is there?" he asked, as they threaded their way through the crowds to the line of glass doors at the main entrance of the block.

"I'm in the car," Tilsett answered. "In the car park nearest this terminal. I brought food and a Thermos.

Thought you might need it. We'll get clear to the North Circular and find a proper park. Can't talk here."

This sounded serious, Vic thought. But he did not attempt to argue. A useless exercise with Uncle Ray. Always had been. So he accepted the leadership he had followed from his boyhood. Without question, that is, until a few weeks ago, when the careful plans had been scattered in a sudden unexpected disaster, from which he had escaped, he hoped, entirely. But had feared the reverse might be true.

The two men did not speak until they were sitting side by side in a lay-by not far from St. Albans. Tilsett handed over a carrier bag with packets of sandwiches in greaseproof paper and a large Thermos flask of coffee.

"All for you," he said. "I've fed this morning."

"Where?"

"Near here. St. Albans. Put up there last night."

"What are you doing down south?"

"Meeting you, you clot. What else?"

"Why?"

"Get on with your breakfast and I'll tell you."

Which he did, lowering Victor's appetite for food as he explained their present need for caution, extreme caution. For the inquiries into the killing of Tan Sunee had, thanks to the patient, Miss Tupper, boiled down to two major possibilities. The murderer could be either of two men, known to have been on the scene of the crime at or near the time it had been committed. The two were Ali Ahmed, the pharmacist and Victor Crawthorne, the architect.

"Here. Wait a bit!" Victor protested. "What about Ray Tilsett, the builder? You and me left that store room together, didn't we? If they're on to me why aren't you up to your neck, too? Aren't they on to you, too?"

Tilsett looked at him sourly.

"You bet they are. But not over the murder. There's another worry. Another nosey parker. Nubb, that chap on the Council. I know we didn't need to tangle with him, but the boss was cocksure as usual. Mr. Know-all Admin. Officer. Thinks he's got them all by the short hairs. Not our Gerald Nubb he hasn't, not by a long chalk."

Crawthorne listened to Uncle Ray's complicated complaints without sympathy. He was concerned, of course, because he'd had his own substantial cut over the success of those contracts that affected the hospitals. But he'd taken the trouble to spend it all in Spain, passing it through various hands before it brought him that marvellous, that fantastic holiday.

"Well, if it's only Nubb, what's the worry?"

"He's been to Newbury."

"So?"

"Got nowhere, of course. But he's a persistent devil. He'll be on to the Law, next."

"But hasn't been yet?"

"Any day now, I should think."

After a brief silence, during which Victor wrapped up the remaining food he no longer wanted and emptied the dregs of his coffee cup out of the car window, Tilsett went on with a description of Miss Tupper's encounter with the two unwanted visitors to her cottage, her ill-advised treatment by them and her return to the Isobel Saunders Hospital.

This fresh misadventure did rouse both anger and fear in the young man.

"Crazy bugger!" he raged. "Who does he think he is? What was the point, anyhow? Old press cuttings? Doubtful pictures? Only draws attention to them!"

"Exactly. Proves they're important."

"Which they can't be."

"How do *you* know?"

Neither of them did, just then. So Tilsett threw the remains of Vic's meal into the bushes, returned the Thermos to its usual pocket in the car and drove on north.

They arrived in Newchester in the late afternoon, where Crawthorne was deposited at his former guest house in the town and Tilsett went back to his own home on the outskirts.

Forewarned by the builder Victor was not surprised to find a message waiting for him. The sender was Detective Superintendent Robertson, who requested an interview as soon as possible, either at the Station or the guest house.

Victor received the message calmly and rang up the Station to say he would call the next day if convenient. Not as convenient as that same evening, he was told. Would he prefer them to call on him? No, he would come down right away, he said.

After telling his landlady he would find an evening meal out, he walked to the Police Station, where he found Robertson waiting for him.

Crawthorne's holiday had done him more good than he realised. Not only had he enjoyed a wealth of new scenes, new sights and sounds, bright colours, hot sun, all of which roused and released in him the drive towards visual art that had been overlaid and nearly extinguished by his training as an architect, and his later slow progression to the safe but essentially boring job he now held. Not only was he able to forget the job itself, but he was out of reach of the man he knew as Uncle Ray. For the first time in his life, apart from two school holiday cruises, he was abroad without Uncle Ray. For three weeks, not the more usual two, he had been complete master of his actions, sole planner from day to day, holder of all the money, accountable to no one but himself. It surprised him to find how utterly independent he was. Questioning this situation further, he decided that he knew the answer. Uncle Ray was taking steps to give him the push. Uncle Ray knew, after the scene at the Isobel Saunders, that he, Victor, was a property too hot to manipulate any longer. So he would be free of Uncle Ray from now on.

In earlier days, even as near as a year ago, the thought of breaking away from Uncle Ray's guidance, which had been complete control, of course, would have made him freeze in panic, before scampering back to shelter. Not so, now.

Bad luck, this new business over Councillor Nubb had driven Uncle Ray to pick him up again with his car and the eats, the explanations and the orders. But he'd shake him off again all right. He'd see to that. He had done well to choose that very pricey hotel. Mopped up the whole of the dangerous bonus. Lucky he'd cashed it in just as soon as he could after that meeting when – After that meeting—

His mind had buried the detail of that meeting from the day it took place, but not deep enough. Well, what of it? Mr. Tilsett, the builder, had given him a share of what was called 'perks'; a prize, or reward, for his part in designing the alterations at the hospital. Nothing else happened in the store room. No slit-eyed, cream-coloured little blackmailer, no—

It was still the story he had told over and over again. It would always be the same story. Only now he was so much better qualified to stick to it in every detail, every repetition. After meeting all those chaps who'd had the power to order their lives as they chose. Not boasting, not throwing their weight about, just confident, just masters of themselves. They'd expected him to behave in the same way, bless them.

All right. Detective Super Robertson should have a basinful of the same: he was bloody well keyed up to it.

Unfortunately for Crawthorne the interview took off in quite a different direction.

"From information received, Mr. Crawthorne," the detective began, "we have reason to believe that your connection with Mr. Tilsett, of the Newchester Builders, is a close and personal one. Is that so?"

"What do you mean by that?" Victor asked, to gain time. This opening had shaken him, but his new attitude to life in general kept his voice steady, calm, unconcerned.

"You have known Mr. Tilsett most of your life, have you not? Is he, in fact, a relative?"

"I call him Uncle Ray, certainly. He used to come up to see us when I was a boy. He's taken an interest all along. I'm very grateful to him as Granny and Grandpa always said I should be."

"I see."

Robertson was a little put out by this engaging frankness, but he pursued the subject further.

"You called Mr. Tilsett uncle. Is he your uncle?"

"I don't really know. My mother told me to call him Uncle Ray the first time I met him, so the name stuck."

"When you grew older did you try to find out more about Uncle Ray?"

"Not really, not before my mother died. I was twelve when that happened. He didn't come to the funeral. That made me wonder. I tried asking Granny, but she shut me up. She said I was *her* son now as well as her grandson. Then Grandpa told me the same thing. They'd adopted me legally."

"With no change of name?"

"Of course not. Mum had been Mrs. Crawthorne."

"Was your father Crawthorne then?"

Victor stiffened. So this was the object of the exercise, his father? All that badgering, all that guff about the grandparents, about Uncle Ray, when he turned up again after the long, unexplained absence, until he left school.

"I never knew my father," he said. "My mother never spoke of him. They must have separated when I was a baby. I was never told that, either. When I did ask Uncle Ray after Mother died, he said she never did divorce him."

"So you were in touch with Mr. Tilsett still in spite of the grandparents' disapproval of him?"

"Who said they disapproved? Oh, well, yes, they warned him off all right. I saw no reason why. He helped to start me on training for an architect. When I was away from home he looked me up. Kept an eye, so to speak. I depended on him to get on."

Robertson began to have a clearer picture of young Crawthorne, Miss Tupper's suspect. He seemed to be genuinely surprised at this rigmarole about his childhood. Better come to the point.

"Did you ever wonder about Uncle Ray's surname? Tilsett was in the papers a lot at one time, wasn't it? You'd be in your twenties then, I think."

So here we were. The dirty nosey parkers! In aid of what, for Christ's sake?

Victor's face grew dark, he frowned, his mouth set in a thin, twisted line.

But he contained his anger. The detective, seeing in one revealing second the countenance that had so frightened Miss Tupper, watched, fascinated, as it melted back into the former good-looking calm. The young man's voice, when he felt able to speak, was only a little hesitant, a little rough.

"I should like to know what all this ancient history is in aid of?" he asked.

For answer Robertson handed him a newspaper cutting. It was dated twelve years before and described the end of the trial of the Black Cat, immediately after he had been found guilty of multiple murder and sentenced to life imprisonment. The picture above the account showed a hostile crowd outside the court.

"I think you will recognise two members of that crowd," the Detective Superintendent said.

Again Crawthorne's face expressed sudden fury, but again he controlled himself, and made no answer. He was remembering his alarm and shock when Uncle Ray showed him the newspaper. He had refused the copy Tilsett had offered him. He had already been told by his so-called uncle that the latter was a cousin of the criminal and that the Cat was his, Victor's, father. Curiosity had taken him to the trial, he had been sickened by the details of the crimes; his only regret was the abolition of the death sentence, then and always thereafter.

"O.K., O.K.," he said at last, staring across the table between him and the Law. "So I was there and Uncle Ray with me and that man, that –" He swallowed back words that meant nothing in the face of those unspeakable crimes, "He was my father. What the hell's the point of bringing it up now? What have *I* done I'd like to know?"

"Nothing as far as we know at present," Robertson told him, "but there is someone who wants to collect, probably to suppress, all knowledge of you and your connection with the Tilsetts."

"That's crazy!"

"Not quite. I'll tell you."

So he explained what had led to the attack on Miss Tupper, her known propensity for collecting cuttings of crime reports.

"We think a fuller knowledge of all the people who were at the Isobel Saunders when a murder was recently committed there may be helpful not only in solving who was the thug that did it but also who are concerned in working a badly set-up corruption racket in Newchester. If you have any information for us, Mr. Crawthorne, or should it be Tilsett—"

"By God it should *not*!" The young man's face was livid. "My grandparents adopted me! I told you! My adoption certificate gives my name as Crawthorne! No other!"

"No birth certificate?"

"That was destroyed."

"Where were you born?"

"I don't know. And I wouldn't tell you if I did!"

Crawthorne got up. He'd had enough, but he felt he'd come through it well, considering.

Detective Superintendent Robertson did not rise. He made a play of setting aside the file from which he had taken the newspaper cutting and drawing towards him a small sheaf of papers pinned together.

"A few more questions, Mr. Crawthorne, if you don't mind. Sit down again, won't you? Will you have a cup of coffee?"

"No," said Victor loudly. "Thanks."

But he did sit down. And he lit a cigarette.

"Your holiday," said Robertson. "Very enjoyable, I'm sure. Very expensive, too."

He read from his papers the name of the hotel and the normal tariff. If Victor was surprised at his knowledge of these facts, he did not show it.

"Very. I'd been saving for it for years. Uncle Ray helped too."

"I'm sure he did. I'm damned sure he did," the Detective Superintendent said fiercely. "How much was your rake-off on those profitable contracts at the hospital?"

This was a mistake. Young Crawthorne was not as simple as he had been. He would not respond now to the bullying direct.

Nor did he. He simply got up again, crushed out his half smoked cigarette and walked away from the table.

The Law had absolutely nothing on him, he knew, but old Uncle Ray looked like being in the soup; well in, if not sunk. And what about that boss, the N.H.S. chap? More burnt fingers. Well, so much the better. Turn the pigs on to that popular failing, corruption, and well away from—

After all, the Paki was still in the nick, waiting for his trial now, wasn't he? Or still on remand? It didn't matter. He was the one surely? Must be. Must be proved to be.

13

Michael Beddoes was cutting his hedge. Mr. Nubb, on the other side of it, watched him with interest and admiration.

"I'm improving," he told the surgeon. "But I haven't got an eye for the shape yet."

"How d'you mean?"

It was difficult to hear the councillor's soft voice above the noise of the cutter, added to passing traffic. It was a fine Sunday morning and people in the road as well as others from the town were all making for the country.

"I just cut the bits that stick out," Mr. Nubb explained. "I don't really appreciate what that will do to the overall shape of the hedge."

Michael laughed. The old boy was his careful, pedantic self in hedge cutting as well as everything else he did.

"Don't worry," he said. "Nature takes over whatever you do. Within reason," he added, knowing his sweeping statement to be wildly untrue.

"You encourage me," Mr. Nubb said. "I must get on with the good work myself."

He moved away and Michael continued to cut, sweep away twigs and leaves and move slowly along.

His thoughts were chiefly on one or two difficult operations he had recently performed, but which now seemed to be giving the patients concerned some measure of confidence in their success, after a week of gloomy complaints that they were feeling worse than before. He had almost been convinced that they were right, which was dispiriting after the efforts he had made for them.

So he did not follow Mr. Nubb's progress back to his own garden, nor notice him come out of his tool shed carrying the new hedge-cutter. It was exactly the same make and size as the surgeon's own, and with it the councillor carried a small aluminium ladder, since being a short man, he needed extra height to attack the top of his own well-grown hedge.

The next thing Michael heard was a shrill scream from the Nubbs' house, followed by Dorothy Nubb's voice calling for help. He switched off his cutter, decided in about one second that it would be quicker to run round in the road than jump into the unknown hazards of the Nubbs' garden. He was there before Dorothy had to stop her cries for want of breath.

Gerald Nubb was lying on the ground. He had fallen, together with the aluminium ladder and was partly underneath it. The fall had knocked the hedge-cutter out of his hand. It lay on the ground nearby. Dorothy stood close beside him, her face ashen, her mouth wide open, ready to scream again for help as soon as her breath returned.

"What happened?" Michael asked quickly, on his knees beside the fallen man, touching him gently with light inquiring hands, ready to turn him over on his back, if safe to do so, because the man had stopped breathing and was in danger.

"That *thing*!" gasped Dorothy. "I always said—"

"Did he drop it and try to catch it? Did he overbalance while he was cutting?"

"No. Not like that at all. I was watching. I was nervous, you know I was."

"Yes, yes."

"He screamed."

"*He* screamed?"

"Yes. He flung his arm out with that thing in his hand, *stuck* to him. Falling shook it off him."

Michael had Mr. Nubb on his back by now, tie and collar loose, and still on his knees was bending to give first aid. But he stretched a hand towards the cutter and pushed Dorothy away from it until he had the battery switched off.

By this time two neighbours had ventured into the garden and Molly Beddoes was leaning out of an upstairs window of their house.

Michael stopped his first aid briefly to shout to her, "Ambulance. Police. My name. This address," before continuing his efforts to start Mr. Nubb's breathing again.

Though it was a Sunday morning the services arrived within ten minutes. By this time, since Beddoes knew the older of the two men in the patrol car, he handed his job over to him. Mr. Nubb was beginning to breathe again in slow uneven gasps. The patrolman changed from mouth to mouth to manual assistance. When an ambulance arrived a few minutes later the men in it took over. Mr. Nubb was carried swiftly on board and oxygen started.

"He's had an electric shock," Michael explained to all the helpers. "That machine on the ground is lethal. It was O.K. yesterday, or last week anyhow. It's the same make as mine. I suggested it to Mr. Nubb and he bought one."

"Have you got the bill, madam?" the patrolman asked Dorothy, which sent her off into the house to find the receipt, helped by Molly Beddoes who had come round after telephoning the two dramatic messages.

"I gave him two lessons on how to use it," Michael went on. "I demonstrated it myself. He knows very little about any electrical device, so I'm positive he hasn't fiddled about with it. But when switched on it's live. So don't try it. I think you ought to wrap it up. You may get an interesting set of fingerprints on it as well as Mr. Nubb's."

The two men looked very doubtful.

"Don't you think it ought to go back to the makers sir?" the older one asked.

"No, I don't. I think you people will deal with it." He paused then said, "Look. I'll come down to the Station with it, if you'll take me. I can explain a lot of things there."

He turned to Molly, who was now beside him, having persuaded Dorothy to rest and have a restoring drink before following her husband to the hospital. He explained what he proposed to do.

"Do you need the gloves for that?" she asked, always practical.

Michael laughed and turning to the two policemen, who were watching, still half suspicious, said, "My rubber gloves. Lucky I had them on when I turned off that thing."

"Very lucky, sir," said the young one solemnly.

"Can't risk getting my hands nicked gardening. Not in my job."

They both looked self-conscious, but made no

answer. Molly took the gloves away. But before she went back to her own house she did go to the tool shed with Dorothy's permission and took away the hedge-cutter's case, wrapping it up as well, in case it, too, might prove useful.

Robertson listened quietly to the surgeon's story of the accident. The hedge-cutter, in a polythene bag, would shortly be on its way to the nearest police forensic laboratory, he had assured Mr. Beddoes: the manufacturers would be contacted the next day. Mr. Nubb had been admitted to the Isobel Saunders Hospital and was making good progress towards recovery. Thanks to the surgeon's prompt action, he said admiringly.

"Never mind that," Michael told him briskly. "The point is rather more important. Who switched the faulty cutter for the good one and why?"

So now Robertson sat back and listened more seriously.

"Nubb was keen to get help over his hedge. He asked my advice and I showed him my cutter. I have it on a flex to the main, because the only hedge I have is the front one and not far from the house. But Mrs. Nubb hated the whole idea and is afraid of electrical gadgets, so he had one with a battery. I showed him how to use it. He was going to ask me to put in a new battery when he needed one."

"So you think someone fiddled with it on purpose. With intent to injure or even kill? Why?" Robertson asked as the surgeon paused.

"I don't know. Nubb kept it on a shelf in his toolshed. Dry shed, very tidy, like everything else of his. Probably switched-on, already-prepared one, for him. Why? Nubb's been worried over goings-on in the Council. Don't ask me. He's told me nothing really, but I can guess. You'd better get the details from him."

"I don't quite understand how you come into it all, Mr. Beddoes, if it concerns Newchester Town Council."

So Michael had to explain his interest in the Isobel Saunders staff, Ali Ahmed's supposed crime, the strange scenes on the second floor of the hospital and his own continuing belief in the Pakistani's innocence, at any rate of murder.

Most of this the Detective Superintendent knew already so Michael Beddoes was able to go home to a late lunch, after which he finished cutting his own hedge, just in time before a call came for him to go to a car crash emergency case in the Newchester General.

Robertson was able to see Mr. Nubb at the Isobel Saunders in the late afternoon. He found the councillor sitting up in bed, demanding to go home immediately. After hearing his story the detective supported this demand and later was able to deliver Mr. Nubb personally to his home and receive from him all the detail he had collected from the various records he had examined. If it occurred to Robertson to wonder at the ease with which the councillor had been able to secure all the relevant papers, he did not remark upon it. The matter, however, needed a great deal of further investigation into the use and misuse of public money. Back to the eighteenth century, weren't we, Robertson thought. He had a taste for history, especially as it related to crime in England, both before and just after the establishment in London of the precursors of a police force. Buying and selling in high places. Never stopped, did it?

Meanwhile he was reminded by Mrs. Nubb, before he left their house, that some villains must have tampered with Gerald's cutter and Mrs. Beddoes, next door, had taken away the horrid thing's case.

"Mr. Beddoes brought us in the cutter itself," Robertson told her.

"But not the case. Mrs. Beddoes has it."

He thanked her and collected it from Molly, annoyed that the two patrol men had done nothing about either the machine or the toolshed. Later, accused of this negligence they were able to give as an excuse for their lack of enthusiasm the big car crash on the bypass that had called Mr. Beddoes to the General. Another instance of the chronic lack of personnel. In spite of a few more cadet recruits Newchester's police force was well below strength.

At about the same time on that Sunday afternoon that the rescued and restored Mr. Nubb was returned to his home, Ray Tilsett called at the guest house in Newchester where Victor was busy getting himself up to date on local news. He was finding that very little of it referred to his own department and was thankful for that. The arrival of his Uncle Ray shattered this growing peace of mind.

"Get your jacket on and come out," the builder said, breathing hard from his rapid climb up to Victor's two rooms on the third floor of the building.

"What's up?" the latter asked. "I was thinking of boiling the kettle for a cuppa. Sit down and I'll give you one."

"No. I've got to talk to you."

Victor stared.

"If they haven't bugged you yet," Tilsett told him,

"they won't be long. Come on, I'm dead serious."

They made their way to the so-called Central Park of Newchester, where Tilsett chose a seat some distance away from others and with open grass, not bushes, behind it. They sat down.

"*Now* let's have it," Crawthorne demanded. They had walked at a furious pace and he had been done out of his afternoon tea, an entirely new habit, not begun in Spain: not the workshop three-thirty tea-break, but the four-thirty to five ritual begun to expand his new self-appointed position in the higher professional ranks.

"I warned his nibs when he was after those newspaper cuttings. Crazy enough and pretty pointless."

"I've never seen them, remember?" Victor was growing angry. "Another thing you've always kept from me."

"Pipe down, you young idiot! The point was he didn't need to see them and if he did, sending in those two thugs of his wasn't the way to do it. Crazy!"

"O.K. O.K., we know all that. Get on!"

"Murder!" breathed Tilsett in a kind of grating whisper. "Might've killed that nosey little so-and-so—"

"I haven't an idea what you're talking about."

Crawthorne sprang to his feet, ready to make off whether Tilsett moved or not, but the older man caught his jacket and hauled him back.

"Sit down, you fool! *Listen!*"

He described the accident to Mr. Nubb in fair detail as it had been told to him on the telephone.

"And for all I know, some bored operator at the exchange will have been listening in and will be tying it all up with the Law by now."

"He lives here, doesn't he?" Crawthorne asked with contempt. "Be on S.T.D., surely?"

As Tilsett did not answer, he got up again, moving out of the other's reach to say, smoothly, "I'm in the clear you know, Uncle Ray. My cut was marked overtime or bonus of some sort. It was you handed out the goodies to get the contracts. If it's blown up in your face that's your own look-out. I'm not getting mixed with it."

"You were mixed into the store room scene," answered Mr. Tilsett, rising slowly to join his young cousin. "You can't deny that. So you can take that smug look off your face—"

But Victor was away by now, striding back along the narrow asphalt paths towards the park entrance, struggling, though his Uncle Ray could not see the effect, to smooth his features free from their furious savage distortion and back to the handsome amiable expression they now much more usually bore.

He went straight back to his rooms. He had not been away more than an hour. A cup of tea at last, perhaps something stronger, was now a necessity, he felt, not an affectation.

But he was thwarted again. A faint noise behind his back made him turn his head from the kettle in time to see a note slide under the door, followed by the sound of retreating footsteps on the stairs.

Even across the room he recognised Mary's writing on the envelope. He started towards the note, but stopped before he reached it. The messenger would be away by now, so there was no hurry. It was the usual routine. No, the old routine, he corrected himself. The old way of letting him know she would be free, alone in her shared flat, waiting for him. He left the note where it was and went back to the kettle, now on the point of boiling.

But when a little later he opened the note after settling himself with his cup, he was stunned by its contents. No message, borne on endearments. An accusation, deadly in its stark meaning.

'Vic, I'm surprised you want to see me again after so long and all that has happened. Perhaps you'll be surprised to know I do not any longer want to see you. So goodbye. And that's for good.'

The wicked look was back on his face as he tore the note across and sprang to the door. But again he clamped down on his anger, bundling it up, driving it out, freeing himself to such good purpose that he went downstairs whistling an old song instead of the latest dreary sentimental moan.

Sister Byrnes opened her flat door at his knock and walked away across her sitting room with her back to him.

Vic stood just inside the closed door, watching her. If she started screeching he'd turn and go and that would indeed be the end of it. If she was only playing jealous again he'd make love to her and prove she had no cause.

So when she did neither, just waited near the window with her back to him, he went across and put his arms round her and began to break down the feeble barrier she had tried to put up. But she would not tell him what she had meant by her note.

Not that he bothered to ask her before he had bedded her, to his great satisfaction and seemingly to hers, too. So why the ice blocks? Why the write off instead of the usual invitation? What was all that in aid of?

"All the rumours," she whispered, which was less than enlightening.

"Such as?"

"Oh, I don't know! I couldn't stand the ward. Those nurses! Hardly spoke to me if they could help it! That Asian! Paki, is he? Still waiting for a trial—"

"Haven't they found it a true bill or whatever old jargon they use?"

"I don't think so. Why can't they find him guilty and have done with it?"

Vic laughed suddenly.

"You *are* a caution! That what you want? Sure he's the one?"

To his surprise she buried her face in his shoulder and cried bitterly. But when he insisted upon hearing some reason for this she would only say he was mocking her and it was serious, no laughing matter.

"I wasn't laughing at the - well, the crime. I was laughing at you wanting to pin it straight and plain on that poor bugger in the drugs department. Is it true he's a worry to the screws, on hunger strike or something?"

"I don't care if he is," said Sister Byrnes harshly, but melted again directly afterwards and wept again, but more gently.

Young Crawthorne went home in a very puzzled frame of mind. If Mary thought she knew more than she should and it was getting her down, the general state of Newchester, with Uncle Ray's low spirits on top, might be getting really unhealthy. The lines were still open to Spain, however, and the state of the kitty was still fine, too.

14

Mr. Nubb's unpleasant experience with his new hedge-cutter, backed by the surgeon's indignation on his behalf, began very soon to show signs of a criminal origin.

To begin with the instrument was not the one bought by Mr. Nubb in Newchester. It had been bought or at least obtained from a very large London store. The store agreed as to the sale but could not offer any information at all about the purchaser.

However, Michael Beddoes' suggestion of a substituted lethal cutter for his original Newchester purchase was correct. Therefore the accident was nothing of the kind; it was a deliberate attack upon the councillor. The motive must surely be his recent searchings into the various accounts of the Council, particularly those related to the local hospitals.

"Cutting their own throats, the idiots," Michael explained to his wife. "If Nubb needed an incentive to complain about this bout of corruption they supplied it. He won't let go now till he's got them all put away, whoever they are."

"Starting with the builders?" Molly asked. "Isn't that the usual form?"

"I'd have thought so. But we're only guessing,

really, because of this string of hospital contracts for building jobs. I wouldn't have thought Tilsett would set up those bloody silly attempts on people who could expose him. I mean Miss Tupper and now poor old Nubb."

"Someone behind Tilsett, then?"

"Looks like it."

In his own mind Michael had already decided that the useless Area Administrator might be the one they wanted, but his own involvement in the Health Service reminded him that he was inevitably biased against this useless official and that it was prudent to leave it to others to expose him. Only in the case of poor Ali Ahmed, now suffering from his self-imposed hunger strike over the delay in bringing his case to court, did he feel he must take any action that seemed possible to relieve him.

The local police, now alerted to strange doings in and near their quiet country town, the case of the faulty hedge-cutter was almost unbelievably stupid in conception and most clumsily carried out. Perhaps it was not intended to kill, only to frighten. If so it was very carelessly controlled, for it could well have been fatal. Of course the plot needed a substituted, doctored instrument. Easy enough to set this up, since Mrs. Nubb was known to have a horror of electrical gadgets in the garden, though she was perfectly used to various washing machines in her kitchen premises. The key for the garden shed hung in the garage on a nail labelled 'shed'. The garage was left open whenever the car was away from home in the daytime.

But to introduce a booby-trap that did not destroy itself as well as its victim, was quite amazing in this day and age, the police felt. They were almost inclined to believe Ray Tilsett's indignant denial of having anything to do with the 'accident' to Mr. Nubb. Tilsett himself was nearly ready to put the whole blame on to Mr. Newbury, where Councillor Nubb had suggested they should look for crooked accounts, with unnatural gains and losses.

In fact the whole corruption racket was on the point of bursting open, when young Crawthorne asked to speak to Robertson again.

Victor had been thinking long and deeply about the present state of mind of Mary Byrnes. There was no doubt she had changed towards him. Though he had not accepted her first denial and had, without much difficulty, insisted upon taking up their relationship again precisely where he had left it when he went to Spain, it did not continue as before.

How could it? The change in her work meant something to him as well as to her. At the most practical level it meant a change in her timetable in detail as well as place in the hospital. She had refused to give him this new timetable.

Her first submission had been complete, but not always since then. She had never again tried to refuse him, but there had been at least one occasion when her open indifference had been very wounding. Victor Crawthorne did not expect to meet indifference to any woman's response to him. He seldom did meet it. But Mary Byrnes had shown him a strange kind of sufferance, not exactly dislike, more like fear, or rather repugnance, that took away all the special pleasure he had enjoyed from her.

And then he had accused her of the change in her and after repeated demands she had suddenly burst out with that cry he could not forget.

"Changed? Why wouldn't I be changed? When I think of what you – When I'm terrified—"

She had begun to sob and hide her face but later, when he had comforted her, she had said in a low, desperate way, "Why can't they try that man, that Indian? Or let him go. If it wasn't him, why keep him? Oh, Vic, I'm so afraid for you! You never see the dangers, ever! Do you? Not ever!"

So that was it! The crooked nurse who'd got what was coming to her. And Mary was scared still for him, because she thought it might've been him – Not that she really cared, but she wanted it settled and herself well out of it, whatever had really happened.

There was a very unattractive smile on Victor's face as he considered his lover's real feelings for him and was chilled by his conclusion. But it gave him a fresh idea, one that might break his dangerous link with Uncle Ray, expose himself to a fresh kind of risk, but bring a suitable helping of sour remorse to Mary, for daring to suspect him. He arranged an interview with Detective Superintendent Robertson.

Detective Sergeant Craig was present as well when Crawthorne was shown into the detective officer's room.

"Does he have to be here?" Victor said, quietly, carefully keeping the insulting tone low.

"Any objection?" asked Robertson.

"Not really. You'll record it anyway, I suppose?"

"If it's worth recording."

Robertson controlled a yawn, but too obviously. Victor grinned. He leaned forward, sitting on the edge of his chair.

"That nurse," he said. "The one that was killed. She was waiting in that store room when Uncle Ray and me went in there that afternoon. She tried to blackmail us."

It was the last thing Robertson expected to hear. Craig murmured "Blimey!" but his superior only drew a long breath and then said quietly, "Tell me exactly what happened. Why you went there at all to begin with."

Crawthorne did so, in a version that disclosed no doubtful money exchanges, only the sudden appearance of the girl and her immediate demands for money.

"You gave her money?"

"Yes."

"How much?"

"What we could spare."

"You had money with you?"

"Mr. Tilsett had his brief case. He will be able to tell you what he gave the girl."

"You seem very uncertain of the amount. Did Mr. Tilsett take it back after you strangled her between you?"

Victor shook his head slowly and sadly.

"Oh, Mr. Robertson, surely you don't think we had anything to do with that girl's death?"

This was true, and the present confession with the complete self-possession of the young man seemed to confirm it, but Robertson was angry, he could not help showing it.

"I think it is very likely your story is a pack of lies from start to finish," he said. "If it was all as innocent as you try to make out why come here with it?"

"The loll – I mean the *money*," said Victor. "You must have found it on her, didn't you? I couldn't put up much, but I'd like it back. Five quid, was what I gave her."

"There was no money, on the body or in the store room."

"Really? He must have nicked it, then."

"Who?"

"That chap you've got, you chump! Sorry, Mr. Robertson, apologies, I'm sure. That poor little Paki you're playing cat and mouse with—"

He stopped. He felt on top of the world; he was scoring with every word, but common sense told him to go no further. The two darkly furious faces before him warned him not to spoil the game. No. Explain. Quietly, carefully, with the deadly logic he had worked out the evening before. Bring this business to the right, safe conclusion, away from Mary's dangerous fears, her purely emotional conclusions.

He told his listeners that the builder and he were on a tour of inspection connected with the forthcoming alterations to the second floor ward. He had given them all that before; it was the new bit that mattered now. He said he and Uncle Ray were startled by the appearance at the store room's inner door of one of the ward nurses. They were not actually aware of her until she spoke, demanding money. Mr. Tilsett had a certain amount of cash with him. In getting out the plans of the alterations he had put this aside on the table. The girl must have seen it.

"There was money between you, then?" Robertson interrupted harshly. "It was nurse Tan Sunee and she had a reputation for blackmail, often attempted and sometimes successful. But you know very well, don't you?"

"I knew it that afternoon." Crawthorne was not a little dashed, but he had a story to finish, so he went on. "She took what Uncle Ray – Mr. Tilsett, gave her, and I produced the fiver and we left her there with it. Mr. Tilsett locked the door. We stood on the landing, talking about what had just happened and whether we ought to report it and if so, who to, and it was then Miss Tupper saw us. I thought—"

"She was balmy. We know all that. And after you had both gone she decided you must have just left the store room, so she went over and found the door open. *Not* locked."

"Because Tan Sunee had gone and unlocked it, all ready for Ali Ahmed, who she had been expecting all along."

"And Mr. Tilsett had gone off with the key, as you told us in your early statements, but the door was open for you to go back later yourself."

So now Victor could play the trump card he had thought up in those sleepless hours.

"Only Miss Tupper had told Sister Byrnes about that open door and Sister had gone along and seen nothing in the outer room and left again, locking up after her. You know I'd left the hospital by five, don't you?"

Robertson could not deny it. He was pretty certain the pharmacist had left the dispensary around five, but not before. Nor had any spare key been available for him as far as they knew. So how had Ali got in? Obvious now, if Crawthorne was speaking the truth at last. Crawthorne told him.

"Tan Sunee opened up again after Sister locked up. Obvious, isn't it? So the Paki's tale is correct, except that when the little blackmailer produced the profits he thought it was for services rendered; her services, you get me. And throttled her in a jealous rage. Right?"

It could be. It fitted the case like a glove, Robertson thought. It was good enough and they ought to have jumped to this conclusion, would have, in fact, if it hadn't been for the old dame's insistence. Shades of that murderer Tilsett. How the public did love a sensational crime and how the media did indulge them. Better not show too much satisfaction, though. This young man's tale was the one piece they needed, but he'd have to explain a bit more about the money in builder Tilsett's brief case. The complete corruption case was unfolding nicely and not on his own plate, thank God.

"Thank you for your assistance, Mr. Crawthorne," he said. "If you will wait a few minutes I will have Sergeant Craig's notes made into a statement for you to sign."

"Will it match the recording?" Victor asked in a maddeningly innocent voice. "I'd like to hear that too before I sign anything."

Ali Ahmed appeared before the magistrates again the following day and was committed for trial at last. He immediately gave up his hunger strike, which had never been so complete as several newspapers and the other media had suggested.

Two days later Michael Beddoes gained permission to see him. He found him pale, haggard, calm, with the resignation of complete despair.

"Before this the police tried to find how I could get into the room after the ward sister locked the door. Now they have proof that the girl was there earlier when the architect and the builder went in. They left her alive and well so she unlocked the door after they left, locking it. She did the same thing after Sister had been to lock it. They say I must have found her alive and well because no one else had been up to the second floor. They say, yes, I speak the truth that the door was unlocked and she was there waiting. But they say I killed her because she was unfaithful with the architect."

Beddoes was shocked, but also exasperated.

"*But not that day*! Impossible!"

"Oh yes, not that day. But she was given money and they say she must have shown me the money and that enraged me."

"I suppose it would if it were true."

Ali's eyes blazed.

"It would not! It would *not*, Mr. Beddoes! I told you it was blackmail and I had grown to hate her for that! I would not care where she got money from or who she blackmailed!"

Michael shook his head. This was no help. He still believed in Ali, but nearly everything he said or did pressed him down a little deeper in the mud of this wretched murder.

The evidence against the Asian still seemed to be purely circumstantial, otherwise the trial would have come much sooner. The interest in the public field had waned, though the police concern, as usual, had gone doggedly on. The prejudice remained rock hard, though kept underground. Newchester had budgeoned into the news again with a very over-ripe piece of corruption, dropping its rottenness from the unpopular over-full ranks of the bureaucracy.

This development was going to cloud Ali's case, Michael thought. The anti-racist groups would be doubtful and keep very quiet, as usual. If he was convicted, they would regret it, but write him off in their minds. He would have fallen too far below like an imaginary, ideal immigrant. He would have behaved like an ordinary, white-skinned bestial criminal, warped by a deprived childhood or mental disease, though perhaps he also had had an even more deprived childhood in Pakistan or even worse mental disability.

The usual load of unhelpful rubbish, Michael thought, unable to sleep that night. The memory of Ali's large, brown, hopeless eyes staring out of a face sickly yellow and drawn, affected him deeply. If the silly lad had only kept his mouth shut from the start, or better still, raised the alarm the moment he found the body. Tan Sunee was expecting him, he acknowledged that. And he had kept the appointment. But she had evidently been a practised little whore. Was he the only client she expected that afternoon? The two men had left the store room soon after four o'clock. Ali would not get away from the dispensary before five at the earliest. But she had opened the door ready for him. Or ready for someone else? *Who arrived?* No one else arrived. No stranger arrived.

A light broke in Michael Beddoes' mind. Before he went to sleep, which he did almost at once, he determined to see Miss Tupper again as soon as possible. There was one answer to his feverish questions that needed answering. Miss Tupper might, with her insatiable curiosity, know the answer.

15

Victor Crawthorne's disclosure led inevitably to a similar confession on the part of the builder. Mr. Tilsett, too, claimed the purest of intention in his dealings with Newchester worthies. He was grateful for their help in granting him civic projects. The jobs he had done for them at competitive prices were all in the way of business. Any reduction in his firm's profits was borne by him personally. Young Crawthorne was perfectly correct in claiming his bonus from Newchester Builders.

"And who told you which jobs were coming up for allocation?" he was asked.

"Naturally I have my ear to the ground," he answered, naming no names.

But Mr. Nubb, showing a bull-dog tenacity in holding on to his well formed suspicions, had no hesitation in giving his belief in Mr. Newbury's part of prime instigator of corruption. This, in turn, helped the police to sort out among the known malefactors living in the underworld of the county town and seen recently in Newchester, a trio of young louts and layabouts they could now pursue with confidence. To follow up these trails and in advance of final action, Mr. Nubb's facts and surmises, his papers giving the results of his own calculations and the details of the attacks upon Miss Tupper and the councillor were sent to the Director of Public Prosecutions, for advice and orders upon how to proceed against the corruption in local government.

"Which is all very well," said Michael Beddoes to Miss Tupper, when he visited her at the hospital, "but do they think you should still be staying here in the hospital?"

"My surgeon does," she answered. "He was horrified when he saw my legs after I came back in."

"I bet he was. But they will be all right, won't they?"

"I think so. I'm allowed to walk about for two hours at a time, but I'm having massage and so on twice a day and he won't let me think of driving the car yet."

"I see. And as poor old Ali is up for trial now, everyone thinks that miserable case is finished and done with."

"But you don't, do you?"

"No. Ali has said all along he went up to the store room after five; he couldn't go before. So after those two men had left, locking up—"

"Oh!" said Miss Tupper. "Of course. They didn't kill Tan Sunee so she unlocked again at once, ready for Ali and that's why I found the door open."

"Perhaps. And after Sister had been to the store room, seen nothing wrong inside and locked up, Tan had again unlocked the door. Tan was still inside waiting, we are led to suppose, so anyone could get in. Someone did and killed her. Who did? The cops have decided it was Ali. They may be right. But who else could it be? Her little friends? The architect? The builder?"

"The tea lady," said Miss Tupper, aghast, and

stopped short, staring at the surgeon. She shook her head from side to side. "I wish I could remember," she went on more calmly. "You know I've had a feeling, ever since they made me meet those two men—"

"The ones who attacked you?"

"No, no. The builder and the architect."

"Yes, go on. But you didn't know them, did you?"

"I felt I had seen the young one's photograph. That was why I got my niece to bring me my newspaper cuttings and the one was like him."

"Which one? Like what?"

She laughed.

"Don't muddle me! You're going too fast. The cutting had them together, outside the court when the murderer, Tilsett, was tried and found guilty. They were Tilsett, the builder, we know now was a cousin and Victor Crawthorne, the murderer's son."

"The police have told you this?"

"Of course. But it wasn't the only photo, the one in the cutting, I mean. I've seen a more recent one, but I can't for the life of me remember where."

"While you were in hospital the first time?"

"Yes, it must have been."

"Somewhere here in the ward, presumably. You didn't leave the ward at all before you went home?"

"That's true. Somewhere in the ward. Another patient's room? There were one or two others in single rooms. We used to wander in and out sometimes, those of us who were up. I never stayed because of not sitting down and marking time if I stopped walking. So *silly*!"

"What about the staff rooms?"

"There wouldn't be *photographs* lying about in the washrooms or the kitchens or the stores surely? Oh," she broke off again as a new idea came to her, "Sister's room!"

"Yes?" said Beddoes quietly, hearing the name he had been waiting for.

"Sister Byrnes had one, no, two photographs on her small desk. There was hardly any room for them. I think there were two."

"But you remember there was one at least. Recognisable?"

"No. I mean one of them must have been of a young man and it must have been the one that reminded me of young Crawthorne. Not at the time, of course. Only afterwards, when I thought I'd seen him somewhere recently. I'm sorry," she said, half laughing. "I must sound like a perfectly crazy old chatterbox."

Michael smiled at her and got up from her bedside.

"On the contrary, Miss Tupper," he assured her. "Compared with most of my own patients you are as clear and lucid as – Now I've mixed my metaphor too badly to finish. No, really you've helped me to straighten my ideas. I still want to help that damn silly little Paki because I don't believe he's capable of killing anyone, except perhaps himself. Mainly because he has a real scientific brain which is very rare in most of the medical students from the east who come here. He would be a real loss if they convict him."

"Could he stay if they don't?"

"Perhaps not in this hospital. He could go home and make a great name for himself in drug research in his own country."

Miss Tupper nodded. She understood his passionate sincerity and admired him for it.

"So you'd like me to find out if Sister Byrnes knows

Mr. Crawthorne well enough to keep a photo of him on her desk? Is that it?"

"That's exactly it," he answered, looking down into the shrewd old eyes lifted towards him.

"She's in Out-Patients now, I believe." Miss Tupper spoke from definite report.

"So I hear."

They shook hands formally.

"Have you seen anything of Tom lately?" she asked, "Phyllis comes regularly, but he's been terribly busy, I hear."

"Yes, I've heard that too."

Mr. Beddoes was gone before she could pin him down to a real answer. But she knew the answer he would give. Poor Tom! Some of his more worth-while clients. To do his best for them, very strictly within the Law at all times. Not easy with what seemed to be going on in Newchester just now. Not her business in any kind of way, of course. She lay back against her pillows and thought over how she should proceed.

Mrs. Walls, with her unappetising tea tray, found her dozing when she arrived half an hour later.

It was not easy to find Sister Byrnes in the Out-Patients department. This was chiefly because the department was divided into several sections. There were two big entrance doors at the back of the Isobel Saunders. These led into the large two-storey block that made up the Out-Patients, having been added some fifty years after the opening of the original charitable gift for the treatment of rural cases from the countryside around Newchester. On one side of the double entrance emergencies, chiefly road accidents, were wheeled in from ambulances to be sorted out, Xrayed or otherwise tested, treated or admitted for treatment. On the other side a mixed bunch of less urgent sufferers sat on benches, waiting for minor treatments and exchanging the fascinating accounts of their ailments. At the far end of the main Out-Patients hall there were two examining rooms where at regular times during the week consultants, or in their absence, suitable registrars, held sessions for patients sent to them personally by their G.P.s.

It took Miss Tupper two half-hour visits to find Miss Byrnes, or rather to locate without making herself known to the nurse. Mary Byrnes had not been to see her since her unexpected return to the hospital, though she had almost at once asked the new Sister Flore to tell her predecessor what had happened to her.

Perhaps Sister Flore had forgotten; perhaps Sister Byrnes had not wanted to come. After the surgeon's visit Miss Tupper took her next walking exercise to the Sister's small office.

It was empty when she got there. The same desk and chair, the same board on the wall immediately behind the desk, the same rows of keys hanging on hooks on the board. The same piles of papers, reports, files, charts, prescription forms, X-ray forms, pathology forms, in a little wooden stand behind the papers. But at the other end of the table where she now remembered quite clearly to have seen two photographs in Byrnes' time, nothing.

Marking time and looking from side to side of the tiny office, Miss Tupper pondered. Until the new, full, cheerful voice of Sister Flore said behind her, "Good gracious, Miss Tupper, you did startle me! Is there anything wrong?"

Miss Tupper was startled in her turn. She swung

round, saying rather loudly, "So you did me! Nothing *wrong*! Why should there be?"

Sister Flore lifted her shoulders in a hopeless gesture, but did not answer. She merely said, "Excuse me!" squeezed past Miss Tupper to gain her chair and sat down.

"I'm sorry," Miss Tupper said.

She meant it. This was not the way to behave to a hard-pressed hospital Sister. She went on in a gentle ingratiating tone, "I came along to ask if you had been able to tell Sister Byrnes I was back in hospital and why. She hasn't been up to see me."

"Oh yes, I told her."

Sister Flore was not a woman to harbour resentment, Miss Tupper thought thankfully, hearing the cheerful voice. She said, "Thank you. Then I suppose she's very busy in her new job. I'd better go down and find her in Out-Patients."

"Yes. You do that, Miss Tupper. But better wait till tomorrow. She goes off duty at six, I think."

So it was not until the following day that Miss Tupper made her first foray into the Out-Patients department and realised, as soon as she had managed to find her way into the central hall of the annexe that she had failed to ask Sister Flore in which part of the busy scene she would be likely to see her former guardian and adviser.

This first encounter with the casualty department was more than unsuccessful; it frightened her. She was unlucky enough to become swept into a line of walking injured from a coach collision. The serious cases had already been rushed through and were on their way in the lifts to the intensive-care units. A few broken limbs and broken heads were under-going rapid and efficient diagnosis in cubicles. But an unhappy, confused number of coach passengers, bruised, cut by glass fragments or merely shocked, pushed ahead with Miss Tupper in their midst, quite unable to make any one of them understand that she had no part in their misfortune.

It was while she was trying with difficulty to force her way out of the queue in a sideways or even backward direction that she heard the well-remembered voice of Sister Byrnes, trying with fluent exasperation to sort out the dazed travellers into some sort of order; at any rate to get them seated, separately, in a row, so that she and the nurses could deal with them as individuals, pass them on, in dressings, bandages, and slings as required, to one of the junior doctors, who could discharge them, if fit, to their relations and homes.

"Not me, Sister!" Miss Tupper cried, above the din. "I only came down to see you and tell you—"

"Holy Mother of God!" said Mary Byrnes, "and me thinking you were beaten up by burglars!"

"I was! I was!" Miss Tupper cried, which so astounded the people surrounding her that they stopped trying to prevent her jumping the queue and let her squeeze out to its edge, where the hospital Sister was trying to help them.

"You are far too busy with this dreadful accident to talk to *me*," Miss Tupper gasped. "I'll come down another time."

As Sister Byrnes only nodded Miss Tupper moved away and went back to the second floor.

But when she got there she remembered what Sister Byrnes had said and when her niece Phyllis came to see her in the afternoon she described the scene in Casualty that morning.

"I told her I'd come down again," she said. "But I'm not sure it would help. I mean, apart from these big accidents which seem to happen so terribly often, the place is obviously always seething; I don't think Sister has anything like her usual office on a ward."

"I should think she must have somewhere to write up case sheets and reports and things," Phyllis suggested. "Trust the bureaucrats in charge now to use all the paper they can organise. They're so good at that; it's the patients they aren't interested in."

"Now, now!" Aunt Amy scolded. "I've been treated wonderfully well. Mr. Beddoes, even, came for a chat, though he isn't my surgeon."

"But Tom is his accountant. I bet he was on about the pharmacist's trial and the naughty councillors gobbling up public money. But I mustn't talk."

"Well, yes, he did talk about all that. He wanted me to find out if Sister Byrnes was a friend of the architect, Crawthorne."

"And did you?"

"No. That accident. I told you. No opportunity. I must try again."

"How d'you mean?"

So Miss Tupper explained about the photographs. She expected her niece to laugh at the roundabout approach but Phyllis did nothing of the sort. She took the idea very seriously, begged her aunt to have nothing to do with it, but to remember what had happened the last time she had tried to interfere with young Crawthorne's identity.

"But that was to do with those councillors and the builder!" Aunt Amy cried. "Even the police have stopped going for the architect. They must have in order to get the murder put up for trial."

"You mean the magistrates found a true bill and stopped remanding Ali Ahmed."

Miss Tupper laughed.

"I think we are both in a proper muddle legally about what's happened," she said. "But I do agree it might be best for me to stop trying to help. I don't really want to help any more. I know I adore drama, but it isn't real true drama, only theatre I love. I saw enough real drama this morning to last me a long, long time."

This mood lasted for the rest of that day. Miss Tupper found she could not rid her mind of the still, grey faces on the stretchers, waiting for a lift to carry them to intensive care, with hope, but no certainty, of survival; the white, pain-racked faces of broken bodies waiting for the relief of an anaesthetic, an immediate future in plaster; the suspended animation of concussion, perhaps a crippled mental state in the years to come.

This was true, living drama and she wanted no part in it, for she understood now that the throttling of one young nurse held the essence of all she had seen and it sickened her.

So when Sister Byrnes came to her room the next afternoon, on the heels of the 'tea lady', Miss Tupper, seeing the familiar face, the deep violet eyes, the neat blue figure, the white Sister's cap, could not fail to shrink from any further wish to speculate upon her reason for coming.

"How nice of you to spare the time to visit me," she said. "I'm sure Mrs. Walls could find you a cuppa, if we asked her nicely."

Mrs. Walls looked as if wild horses would not persuade her to respond nicely however they proposed such a thing, but Sister Byrnes spared her the effort.

"No thanks, Mrs. Walls," she said cheerfully. "Mustn't stay above a minute."

She embarked on a list of questions about Miss Tupper's legs, giving the old lady barely time to answer. When she came to an end and was satisfied that the operation result had been saved and the patient very soon to leave for home, perhaps staying with her niece again for a few days, she jumped up, satisfied that no danger could come from this quarter, in spite of the nasty shock she had felt the day before in Out-Patients.

"But you mustn't run away without telling me about yourself," Miss Tupper said, soothed by the other's solicitude and quite unaware that this was exactly what she intended.

Sister Byrnes sank on to her chair again but stayed poised to go at any hint of danger.

It came almost at once.

"I've missed you," Miss Tupper said, smiling, "very much. Your little room's quite different. Sister Flore has more paper on the table and none of those cosy photographs."

Sister Byrnes held on to the sides of her chair.

"Photographs?" she asked, in a voice that should have warned Miss Tupper, but did not. Her re-born euphoria, her lively curiosity, her love of dramatic situation, swept back in full force.

"Yes, my dear. A grand, elderly couple; parents, were they? And the young man, dark, smiling, the boy-friend, is it? Reminding me so much of—"

"No!" Mary Byrnes was up now, glaring, but terrified. "You're wrong! Imagining! I haven't got a boy-friend! How dare you!"

She was choking with rage and fear and shame at her own loss of control, of any kind of sense.

"I'm sorry," Miss Tupper said. "I must be quite mistaken. How very silly of me! Broken off, is it? Oh, do forgive me!"

"You bloody, silly, nosey old cow!" cried Sister Byrnes and rushed out of the room.

"A Celtic fluency," Miss Tupper murmured to herself. "Did she imagine no one ever looked at her photographs when she had them out on her table? I wasn't the only walking patient."

16

Miss Tupper was shaken. It was so unlike the usually gentle Mary Byrnes to use such vulgar expressions, quite apart from the silly denial, the passion expressed in her voice and in every feature of her thin, pale face. For it all agreed with the suspicions, now confirmed, that had filled Aunt Amy's mind since the visit of Michael Beddoes. She could tell the surgeon now that yes, Sister Byrnes had kept a photograph of the young architect on the little table in her office in the ward. Also that she had denied this with fury, had been very much upset at the suggestion, which therefore must be true.

So, Miss Tupper continued in her own mind, when she herself went to Sister Byrnes to tell her of the two men on the landing, of the agitation of one of them, his resemblance to the Cat of hideous memory, and of the open door of the store room, all this meant a great deal more to the nurse than she could have imagined at the time.

What, precisely, must it have meant to the nurse? Firstly, that when the builder and the architect went to the store room together, presumably on hospital business, Tan Sunee must have been there already, but had not yet unlocked the door, for they had used a key for that. But when they left, locking the door behind them (for the builder had returned the key to the workshop), the little nurse had at once unlocked it. It was still unlocked when Sister Byrnes went there, following her report. This had always been the explanation.

But had Tan Sunee, presumably still there, waiting perhaps for Ali Ahmed, again unlocked it after Sister had taken a swift look around and seen nothing?

Surely this was possible. But if so, why the agitation? Could it be that Sister Byrnes suspected the arrival, not of Ali Ahmed but of Victor Crawthorne? Had there not been rumours of his fairly frequent visits to the second floor? To see the nurses, or one of the nurses? Or to see Mary Byrnes?

Either, or perhaps – dreadful thought – both? In which case, Miss Tupper decided, poor Byrnes was afraid he might have killed the nurse and hence her agitation, being well aware of Tan's habits and suspecting she must have missed her and that locking the door was useless and either Ali or Victor would have found it open.

Or else? Or else what? Miss Tupper felt her mind clouding over; she was becoming confused. But an even more sinister thought had come pushing its way in, compounded of her own persistent inquiry and Sister's passionate despair.

Supposing the nurse had been deeply affected by her, Amy Tupper's sudden fright, and going to the store room to satisfy her own fears, had found Tan Sunee dead, the door still open and had realised that anyone could have gone in. So then, Sister had left again at once, unable to give the terrible news, because she must protect her own love, even if he had betrayed her with the foreigner.

Miss Tupper lay still, quite frightened by the vivid workings of her imagination. It did make a most satisfactory melodrama, but she felt she must scold herself for playing a theatre game with a situation so genuinely tragic.

In any case so lamentable. She must confide her dire conclusions to others; it was not safe with her. She would tell Phyllis and Tom. They would be sure to tell Mr. Beddoes. Perhaps she had better tell Detective Superintendent Robertson.

Neither her niece nor her husband was in. They had gone to the theatre, the baby-sitter said. She left a message to say she had called and it was important, but could wait till morning.

The Police Station told her neither of the detectives was there. Detective Sergeant Craig was off duty. Detective Superintendent Robertson was out, but expected back. She left a message for him, too. It was important and she thought he ought to see her as soon as possible.

Both these moves on Miss Tupper's part had been foreseen by Mary Byrnes. When, that evening, Victor arrived on her doorstep, she greeted him with renewed agitation that did nothing to restore the ardour he had felt for her before his holiday in Spain.

"What's eating you *now*?" he cried in very natural exasperation. He took his arms from round her and moving away to the only armchair in her small sitting room, sat moodily sideways in it, both legs over one of the arms, spilling cigarette ash on the carpet.

"It's that woman Tupper, who's been making the trouble all along," she said grudgingly.

He shook his head at her, half laughing.

"But I've sewn it up nice and tight," he said, showing his fine white teeth at her. "Spilled the blackmail that little devil tried on. So the pigs think she opened the store room door just when and how she wanted. They've got their case against the Paki, which is how they wanted it all along. Me and Uncle Ray's sitting pretty."

"Come off it! Sitting pretty, indeed! Sitting on a muck heap from what I've heard. The Council up to their necks and poor little Mr. Nubb—"

"They're bonkers! I've warned Uncle Ray. He can count me out from now on."

"Can he do that, even if he wants to? You must be in that racket, Vic. Didn't I warn you?"

Crawthorne reached a hand down to grind out the stub of his cigarette on the floor, before taking another from his pocket and lighting it. The sickly smell of cannabis began to float through the room.

"Lay off," he said, in the new quiet voice she had begun to fear. "You yap like a starved bitch on heat. No!" he said, with one fierce dark look that dried her mouth. "I don't want to hear it. I've got it all sewn up. When they've put that little runt away for a lifer, I'm off out of this blasted country."

She had known her hold was slipping. She supposed he had the money. if he had given it in blackmail, he must have taken it back, of course. He would. Part of his cut? Well, if he wouldn't be warned—

As for Victor, he saw through Mary's would-be interfering and he wasn't having any of it. Only make a muck-up of his own line of action. As for taking it out of the old girl in the ward – (back there and serve her right) – there would be none of that again, so Mary needn't think it.

He swung his legs down and stood up.

"I'm for the off," he said. "Be seeing you."

Or more probably not, he thought. Getting a bit risky. Anyway, he could do without wet blankets of her sort. Not up to his new style. He'd come on a lot since Spain. She hadn't taken account of that.

Mary watched him go. So this was what she had worked and slaved and suffered for! She was dry-eyed, bitterness in her mind and heart. And the thirst for revenge, deep, tribal, soaking up the tears.

Crawthorne's news about Tan Sunee had alone done more than bring about the committal of Ali Ahmed for trial at the Crown Court. In order to make that trial effective, Detective Superintendent Robertson set about arranging the material evidence in proper order. This new story, revealing the girl's presence while the two men were in the store room, was now proved. The builder had confirmed it; both had alibis for the rest of that afternoon and evening. Besides Ali Ahmed had himself confessed to seeing the body that afternoon soon after five.

Of course it was remotely possible that the younger man's account was false, but Robertson thought this unlikely. He thought he was reading the young man correctly. He thought that Crawthorne had taken his cut from the contracts and converted it rapidly into cash, however it had been paid. There were several ways of doing this in the modern world of business, where the false ran hand in hand with the true, the dishonest juggled with the straight, complicated criminal operations ran like underground rivers, to surface as innocent bank balances.

Young Crawthorne had spent his prize at once, lavishly, in Spain. Tilsett was busy covering his own deals with a lard of generosity, while passing the corruption motive back to the Area Administrator. Newbury was now a confused, very frightened operator. Two rough types, seen about the pubs in Newchester recently, had since left the district. But they had left recognisable traces in Miss Tupper's country home and in Mr. Nubb's toolshed. They would be traced and picked up in due course.

For actual physical traces of the murder in the store room the site had been only too productive. There were fingerprints, there for legitimate reasons, of all the known actors in the scenes played there, including those of Miss Tupper, Sister Byrnes, and also the little friends and colleagues of Tan Sunee. It had taken time and patience to establish the long list, with an overall result that was worthless.

These prints had been taken chiefly from the doors, windowsills, table, chairs and cupboards. In the inner room, the 'love-nest', as Sergeant Craig would call it with dreary facetiousness, the only furnishing was a heap of dusty cushions of various shape, size and colour, piled at one side. The girl's body had been lying upon this pile when found. Later tests had been made on the covers of these cushions, in a search for the origin of several stains found there.

Robertson turned over the pages of the reports that had come in from the County Forensic Laboratory. Saliva, semen, sweat, tea, coffee, cannabis, sputum. All the ingredients of a right sordid little brothel, the detective thought.

And the cushions themselves? Where had they come from? Not supplied by the N.H.S. Besides, most of them were from cheap stores in the town. Their origin was revealed when the outer covers were taken off for analysis of the stains.

Inquiries soon found the answer. The nurses did not mind telling the truth of this. They had been provided with a rest room for themselves in the geriatric part of the ward. It had several wicker armchairs; they preferred to sit at ground level and had asked for poufs, not granted. So they had bought cheap cushions for the wicker chairs and when the gaudy rubbish that covered them had not survived their new use, had covered them with any old pieces of material they could lay their hands on.

These pieces of material were of different kinds, mostly consisting of discarded outdoor clothes of the nurses themselves. They wore European blouses and skirts, both long and short, as a rule. Some of them wore trousers, a more normal copy of their national costume, but of course not suitable for turning into cushion covers.

It was in tracing the origin of these materials, to discover where the girls had found them, that a line of research began at the forensic laboratory that led directly to Detective Superintendent Robertson's file.

A faded plain mid-blue cotton, or rather acrylic material had come, not from any of the local cheap multiple stores in Newchester, but from the only old-fashioned draper in the town. This shop prided itself upon its superior linens and cottons and upon stocking their nearest equivalents in the new, chemical fabrics, almost as superior to look at and better in use because they did not crush or fade or shrink and would drip-dry in a couple of hours. And all at about half the price the old-fashioned materials had now reached with inflation.

All this Detective Sergeant Craig learned when Robertson sent him to the draper concerned. The detective saw the manager in his office and produced the grubby blue cushion cover, returned from the laboratory to form an exhibit, if needed, at Ali Ahmed's trial.

"As you see, no trace of fading, officer," the manager said proudly, returning the specimen and wiping his fingers on a duster he took from a drawer in his desk.

"Quite so, sir," answered Craig. "We are anxious to discover if possible, whether this particular piece, which you say you stock, was actually bought here."

It was a tall order and he knew it. But the manager was on his mettle. If he could make the identification his assistance would be acknowledged by the police, which meant useful publicity for his shop. It was hard enough to keep up to date these days in a town like Newchester.

He nodded gravely and pressing a button on his desk sent his secretary to find a Mrs. Smith.

"My only assistant of real experience in the cottons and linens," he said. "The girls take no interest at all in the goods. Or in the customers, either."

Mrs. Smith was at first inclined to be annoyed.

"It's so very long since we had regular customers, sir, and customers with accounts here who were looking for the article they wanted, without troubling themselves over the price—"

"We do have a few," the manager interrupted. "It is no criticism of *you*, Mrs. Smith, as I'm sure you know."

"If," Craig put in, "you could suggest what kind of person would buy this kind of material, or what for? You see, we think it may have been a worker at the hospital."

"*Hospital?*" Mrs. Smith was astonished. "*Worker?*"

"Not the nurses," Craig hurried on. "They have uniforms supplied, of course. Nor the overalls, white for most of the medical jobs, dark green for the others. Actually we think this cushion cover was made of old material belonging to or given to or found by some of the hospital nurses."

Mrs. Smith paused to take all this in. Then she said slowly, having discarded it as plain nonsense, "If you're asking me if I know of anyone at one of the hospitals who buys this sort of fabric then I do know someone and we have her on our books, sir," she said, turning to the manager. "It's a Miss Byrnes and she's had two dress lengths in the last year. I've seen her at the Isobel Saunders, but we have her home address on our books. That I do know, because we delivered an order to her flat."

Taking back his grubby specimen Craig expressed thanks, said he knew Miss Byrnes, also her home address, and left. The manager and his assistant watched him go in silence.

Mrs. Smith said, "If he knows her, why hasn't he asked her to her face about the cushion, I wonder? And how did he know we stocked that material?"

The manager shook his head.

"Well, he'll ask her now, I expect," he said slowly.

Which was what Craig proposed to Robertson must be his next assignment. But the Detective Superintendent hesitated. For he had had a call from the forensic laboratory and he was waiting for his Sergeant's return before going off there. His thoughts had led him to exactly the point reached by Michael Beddoes and later, in much the same form, by Miss Tupper.

For a new light had been cast on the finger nail contents gleaned from the dead nurse. Overlooked at first, these fragments of cotton appeared now to have come from the cushion cover recently returned. To confirm this they wanted to have it back at once. Robertson promised to bring it in person.

He sent Craig off duty with directions to leave Sister Byrnes in peace, but to meet him at the Isobel Saunders that evening after eight.

So neither of them was at the Police Station when Miss Tupper's message came. And neither of them called at Miss Byrnes's flat, to find it in darkness and the nurse not at home.

17

Detective Sergeant Craig was bored. He felt himself ill-used, most unjustly. He did not resent his position of legman in this long, surprisingly difficult case. But having carried out his mission to the draper's shop and gained a very satisfactory result over the provenance of the 'love nest' cushion, he had looked forward to concluding it with a final visit to the hospital to find Sister Byrnes and confirm that she had made a present of an old dress to the nurses in her former ward.

But not a bit of it. His chief had been pleased, but not markedly so. He had been tense, almost off-handed, as if some new fact or new aspect of one already before them, had suddenly arrived to absorb his full attention. And he had not explained a word of it. Further action was for himself alone, so he, the assistant, could go chase himself till later on that evening.

Hardly good enough, Craig grumbled on to himself. However, he was due for a break and a meal, so that was what he did next. Then, his energy and common sense fully restored, he made his way to the Isobel Saunders, to inquire in the Out-Patient department for Sister Byrnes.

She was not there, he was told. She had gone off duty at six o'clock and was probably at home. But further inquiries and searches found that though her umbrella was not on its hook, her uniform coat was there and her locker below the hook was locked, so presumably her handbag was still in it. There had been a shower of rain an hour earlier, so perhaps Sister had taken the umbrella to cross the courtyard to the main building or the old annexe, but was still somewhere in the hospital.

In the second floor ward the little smooth-faced nurses in their neat green uniforms were there as before. Craig could not decide if he had really seen any single one of them before. Nor, from their impassive faces, whether any of them recognised him either. He realised, almost at once, that they were not going to help him in any way at all. They were not going to disclose any knowledge of English, however much or little they had learned. They were not going to tell him where they had found the blue material to cover their cushion. They were not going to agree that it came as a present from Sister Byrnes. Perhaps they would not even agree that they had worked for that particular Sister. He could not accuse them of lying. He did not really know if he had ever seen one of them before that evening.

He took his difficulty, with apologies and some hesitation, to Sister Flore. She listened sympathetically, looking at her watch as she spoke.

"I don't think I can help you," she said. "I'm off duty myself in a few minutes. I haven't seen Mary Byrnes at all for a couple of days. I think she finds Out-Patients very hard work after this ward. It gets worse, you know. So many people think they can use us as a free chemist's shop for anything they can get at Boot's; just for the asking, no doctor's letter or even a few questions, far less a prescription. They don't mind the waiting. They're used to queues for the dole and the social security and pensions and everything else. Standing in queues or pickets or marching in demos is all the exercise the feebler half of the population takes."

She spoke bitterly and impatiently; it was clear that she had no use for Craig's question. Nor did she consider herself involved in it or its implications. She was eager to be off.

But he could not let her go, leaving him there, already a little late back at the Station without any excuse for his delay.

"Just one thing, Sister," he pleaded, "before you go. Is Miss Tupper still here, still in the ward?"

"Miss Tupper? Oh yes, *she's* still with us."

Sister Flore was now looking more amused than annoyed.

"Wonderful old girl, I must say. Now, I've got to go. You go and talk to her, Sergeant. Always full of ideas, never at a loss for a surprise. We shall miss her when she goes to her niece tomorrow."

"She's off then, is she?" said Craig.

He was still staring at the nurse's wrist watch, disclosed when she had pushed up her loose forearm sleeve. As she pulled it down she drew off both the short forearm sleeves and tucked them into her wide apron pocket. The uniform sleeves, bodice and skirt, above and below the white appendages, were blue, of the shade he had been concentrated upon for much of that day.

He said nothing to Sister Flore as he thanked her and walked away to Miss Tupper's room. But after the old lady had welcomed him and told him to sit down he asked at once, "Miss Tupper, I see that Sister Flore is wearing a *blue* uniform. Is this a new idea?"

She laughed.

"Good heavens, no. Always blue for the Sisters. Green for the nurses."

"I know nurses have green. Don't know why I never noticed Sister was different. Brighter blue, perhaps, on Sister Byrnes."

"Sister Flore wears the official uniform. Same material as the nurses, only blue, not green."

"And Sister Byrnes?" He was aware that his voice had grated in his growing excitement.

"Oh, she's very particular. Well, it was after they had trouble in the laundry departments a few years back. Couldn't get the Health Service uniforms washed or cleaned. Sister Byrnes told me once, when I said she always looked so neat and fresh."

"Told you *what*, Miss Tupper?" Craig knew what was coming and began to see what it would mean.

"Why, that she got some material the same colour as the official sort and had a couple of uniforms made for herself which she could drip-dry at home. It isn't the first time nurses have been driven to look after themselves when the unions try to boss the Service."

"My *God*!" whispered Craig, paralysed for a second by all this could mean, *must mean*, in the light of the forensic findings.

And he was due back at the Station at this moment, with his chief waiting for him, who ought to be here, where—

"Is that so?" asked Mary Byrnes, from the door.

She was standing there, neat as usual, in her blue uniform, self-supplied, holding a small covered dish in her right hand.

She was answering Miss Tupper's account of her dress and there was a look on her face, not seen by

Craig, who had his back to her, that drove the patient to cry out quickly, "Don't go, officer! Don't leave me!"

"Back in a minute!" he called from the door and was gone. To find a telephone and call Robertson, then get back to the ward to guard this new quarry.

He did not know that his chief had already got Miss Tupper's message and was on his way to the hospital. Nor that the quarry was no longer the sought after, the pursued, but the pursuer, the avenger.

Sister Byrnes stood aside to let him go, smiling in a way that did nothing to reassure Miss Tupper. For the latter, though she knew nothing about the forensic laboratory and its tests, did know quite well the conclusion Craig had reached from her answers to his questions, for it must be the same as her own. Sister Byrnes's appearance only too fearsomely confirmed it. The little covered tray terrified her.

"Why, Sister!" she exclaimed, hearing her voice shake a little. "Have you forgiven me? When you left me the last time—"

"I cursed you for an interfering old bitch, didn't I?" the nurse said, moving a little nearer. "So you have to remind me, don't you? Have you always been like this, interfering, prying, bullying—? Driving folk out of their wits?"

She must be mad, Miss Tupper thought, and I never suspected it till now. Oh, why has that policeman gone away when he was most needed? How am I to get out of this room? Ring my bell? No one will come. Sister Flore must be off duty by now. The nurses won't pay any attention. Thank goodness, I'm half dressed. If I can get out of the room I can run. I can try to run.

"No, Sister," she said, calmly, not pleading, stating

facts. "I have never been like that. I relied on you for help and guidance, I did what you told me. You were wonderful. I have missed you very much since I came back. Sister Flore—"

She went on chattering madly about her treatment and her operation and the hospital routine, while slowly, carefully, she put aside the single blanket that covered her legs and tensed herself, ready to slide to her feet when she felt she had gathered sufficient strength.

She succeeded at first. She did move fast enough to gain an upright stance and that on the opposite side of the bed to the distraught nurse, whose agitation was plainly rising, who had planted her little covered receptacle on the top of the bedside locker and removed from it a loaded hypodermic needle. She broke into Miss Tupper's frightened monologue with a harsh order.

"Stop that drivel! Get back on the bed. I am here to give you your injection."

"I don't have any injections now!"

"You will have one tonight. This one."

"I will not. I am leaving this hospital." She had a quick thought. "They are coming for me any minute now."

Sister Byrnes swung round to look at the door and Miss Tupper seized the moment to push the bed, on its well-oiled movable castors across the other's path, to hem her in.

It could be a temporary move only, but might have afforded the old lady an opportunity to reach the door. But Aunt Amy's legs were still too feeble and their muscles too ill-used and elderly to respond to sudden calls for athletic action. She plunged in the right direction, tripped over the edge of the blanket she had thrown from her, toppled in the wrong direction and found herself saved from falling by a well remembered, blue-clad arm.

"Steady, then!" Sister Byrnes said, easing her declared enemy, her planned victim, to a seat on the end of the bed. "Rest now, while I get your injection ready."

Aunt Amy began to cry. She was lamenting not only her present plight and the inevitable end she foresaw awaiting her, but her failure to understand this woman's mind, that must have begun to crumble so many weeks ago. *She* understood, but did those painstaking police officers? Was it all going wrong now, so near to the right solution, the dreadful, timeless end to jealousy, as old, as certain, as passionately deadly, as life itself?

She was not willing to give in; she was prepared to fight on. She flung herself sideways to snatch up the fallen blanket from the floor and thrust it between herself and her attacker. She knew the syringe and its contents had gone at an early stage and was thankful for that, even if the next attempt was a determined effort to smother her with a couple of her pillows.

And then, as faintness swept over her, she heard a fresh sound in the room. A bang, as the flimsy partition door swung open and back; a roar, deep, wholly masculine, a wild scream from Sister Byrnes and the pressure on her relaxed completely, but the sounds of struggle continued.

Miss Tupper pushed herself free and sat up. Two figures writhed together on the floor; the nurse was on the ground; kneeling over her, his hands round her throat, his face—

"Stop!" shrieked Miss Tupper, forcing herself to

move. "Let go, damn you! Damn you – CAT! – Devil! Wicked, black devil! —"

Victor, beside himself with fury, was almost beyond recall, but not quite. The voice he now heard was the voice of his grandmother, the voice that had assailed him in his childhood every time his ungovernable temper had broken loose in dangerous earnest. Every victory over it that she had secured for him, every effort he had been making of late, came to save him now. His hands obeyed the voice of Miss Tupper, though his passion still raged.

"Take your hands away! Get up! Leave her alone! Get up!"

She was hitting him in the face, about the head, with a hard-edged book off her bed-table. He had to ward it off, to clutch it, snatch it from her.

"Get up and give me back my book!" Aunt Amy ordered.

He was speechless, but he did as he was told. Afterwards she was asked if she had not been afraid he might attack her instead, but such a thing had not occurred to either of them at any time.

"Why did you attack her?" Aunt Amy demanded.

"She was killing you."

"Why did that make you try to kill her?"

He did not answer this, but looked away at the nurse, who was twisting about on the floor, choking and spitting and moaning her distress.

Though the noise from their part of the ward had for some time been quite considerable, not a single nurse appeared to discover what it was all about. Not a doctor. Not a porter. Until Detective Suprintendent Robertson with Detective Sergeant Craig got out of the lift on the second floor and hearing Miss Tupper's verbal attack, delivered in ringing tones trained to reach the back of the theatre gallery and the furthest point of the pit, and ran as fast as they could to her room. They found a scene of exhausted violence and stood staring at it.

Miss Tupper, in a petticoat over underclothes, was sitting on the side of the bed, which was pulled askew with the bedclothes heaped at one end.

Sister Byrnes, in uniform, without her white half-sleeves, her white collar crumpled and torn, her blue skirts round her thighs, her Sister's cap on the floor beside her, crouched near the bed, still coughing and moaning. While Victor Crawthorne, his clothes only slightly disordered, his large hands dangling, an embarrassed smile on his face, leaned in a protective way over Aunt Amy.

18

Two weeks later Miss Tupper was still living with the Hunts on the outskirts of Newchester. There was much going on that concerned her and her presence there was not only convenient but highly desirable. Besides, Phyllis was by now a practised hand at thwarting, while mollifying, the media in all its forms. At her country cottage Aunt Amy would not have been able to cope.

She herself was happy enough to submit. Secretly she wondered if she would ever be able to face living alone again. Her final experience in the exposure of Sister Byrnes had been too real, far too appallingly real. Certainly she had guessed, as had Michael and Victor and the police pair, that Sister herself had left the store room door open when she was supposed to have locked it again. But she had thought the nurse had done so to protect her lover. It was the detective who knew, from the discovery of blue threads under the victim's finger nails, traced to those self-made uniforms, that the nurse, more jealous than protective, had killed her rival instead.

"She doesn't deny it," Robertson had explained to Miss Tupper. "Says she found the girl, shaky but vicious, she says, furious at sight of her, waving bank notes in her face, saying Vic had given them for services rendered and was laughing at her, Mary Byrnes. So she took the money and strangled the girl. She burned the notes at her flat that evening."

"There is no real defence then, is there?" said Miss Tupper. "In this country?"

"Sympathy, though. Provocation. Lying foreigner. No morals. Lax discipline. The Senior Nursing Officer is having a sticky patch, I believe. There's this other case."

He refused to discuss that. But Mr. Nubb was not so professionally reticent. He was sorry for those colleagues who had been such silly mugs, as he called them. But it had been really quite impossible to bring anything actually criminal against Mr. Tilsett, certainly not against his company. Newbury, on the other hand, was suspended at once by Sir Frank Pelman, who seemed to recover all his old grasp of affairs with the disappearance, not replaced, of the Area Administrator and the absorption of that office, shedding redundant secretaries and officials like autumn leaves, into his own establishment. Temporarily, it was said. But, hopefully, permanent.

Ali Ahmed did not, of course, have to stand a trial. On the contrary he was released from prison a few hours after Sister Byrnes was arrested. The charge of murder against him was dropped. For a time a much lesser charge of concealment of a death was considered, but in fact of his acknowledged, but unavoidable sufferings, it was dropped as well.

His suspension from his job at the hospital dispensary was also dropped, but he did not go back to work there, which was not surprising. He resigned from the post and faded into the body of his compatriots, who had supported him with money and kindness and religious exhortation and advice, during his misery in prison.

But he was still grateful to Beddoes, who tried to keep in touch with him, not very successfully.

"I think he's been put off trying to make out in this country," Michael explained to Tom. "He'll never forget this experience. He thinks the majority here hate his guts simply for taking one of their good jobs, regardless of his brains in getting it. Perhaps because he is cleverer than most chaps in the job. I only hope he gets into some kind of chemical research in his own country, which is where he belongs – research, I mean."

"Why not one of our big drug firms with branches there?" suggested Tom.

"That's an idea. But no good telling him to go for it. They'll have to ask him."

"Too true."

As for Victor Crawthorne, Aunt Amy insisted upon asking him to visit her, together with his Uncle Ray.

"He saved my life," she explained to Phyllis, who even now did not want to believe this. "He is an immoral young show-off and he uses cannabis when he thinks it won't be noticed. He treated poor Byrnes abominably, sending her off her head like that. But he didn't kill her and I was wrong about him and got him into all that bad trouble that might have ditched him, together with that old rogue in the building trade."

So Mr. Tilsett and Victor came to tea at the Hunts' house and Phyllis gave them thin bread-and-butter and honey, and paste sandwiches and a home-made cake. A real Edwardian tea of the kind Aunt Amy had been used to in her girlhood.

Uncle Ray was not very happy in these circumstances, that broke into his normal office hours and filled his stomach far too soon after a business lunch at midday.

Vic, on the other hand, was both elated and soothed. He had, quite honestly, done his best to help the old girl before he lost his temper with Mary. He had helped to save her from Mary and she had saved him from throttling that jealous, hysterical judy. He felt they were quits, equal in service to one another. Afternoon tea, old-fashioned upper class tea, the kind his grandmother in the north had sometimes laid on for her friends, brought him back again to the way he must continue to follow when he had got over the present trouble, turned the present awkward corner.

Miss Tupper put the seal on it, but not quite as he expected.

"Victor," she said, when the tea was over and they had gone back into the sitting room, leaving Phyllis to clear up the table. "I don't know if you are liable for any charges of fraud, as Mr. Tilsett may be—"

"Now look here, madam," the builder began, but she waved an imperious hand at him and he subsided.

She went on, "I hope nothing will, and the police must be grateful to you in more ways than one. But if you are not to follow the dreadful path of your father you have got to control that appalling temper."

It was a shock, a direct push, so to speak, from the top of the tower, from the view of the world, to the darkness of the basement dungeon. But he took it well. In his new conception of himself there was no place for hideous deeds. Besides—

"In the past," Aunt Amy continued, "young men with uncontrollable tempers could go away from this crowded island to the wilder parts of the empire. We have no empire now and no place for the wild young men. But the world is still there and for people like you some spot where energy and skill and talent – you have all of those – you have your profession – are welcome and tempers are normal occurrences and have normal outlets."

Mr. Tilsett was shocked. She couldn't really be telling the lad to go away where he could kill or be killed and it wouldn't make a blind bit of difference.

"I've done my best for years to keep him off the gallows," he protested, "before they changed the rules, more's the pity."

"He can't help his inheritance," Miss Tupper insisted. "He has his father's temper, but he can learn to keep it within bounds."

"Which he hasn't yet," Mr. Tilsett continued. "Why, he'd have finished that little blackmailer if I hadn't stopped him."

Miss Tupper froze. She was speechless.

"He had her by the neck. I hit him. I made him give her back the money and we left her."

Victor hung his head. The bad memory came back to him again. She had been so small, the neck so thin, the little bones that he was squeezing seemed to be squashing together like caramel. He'd never forget it. Worse than Mary. She was fighting back and then the other memory had weakened him, too. She'd have broken free.

Miss Tupper was recovering.

"So *you* saved him that time, Mr. Tilsett! You say there were other times before that?"

"From causing bad injury, yes. Not from plain murder before."

"And you left, locking the door. So Tan Sunee was well enough recovered to open it at once."

Mr. Tilsett drew a long breath and shook his head.

"I left it open," he said, "in case she wanted help. But I told Vic I'd locked it, in case he got ideas about going back."

Vic lifted his head to look at Miss Tupper.

"Mary killed her," he said. "She had Mary's dress material under her fingernails."

Miss Tupper was still amazed. She had been right from the start and wrong from the start. With her theatrical glee she was no better than the other two.

"We three are all guilty," she said. "All killers."

"Rubbish!" Vic said and Uncle Ray agreed.

"We are all human," Aunt Amy said. "Killers."

*If you have enjoyed this book, you might
wish to join the Walker British Mystery Society.*

*For information, please send a postcard or
letter to:*

Paperback Mystery Editor

**Walker & Company
720 Fifth Avenue
New York, NY 10019**